"Do you need love, Uncle Rick?"

"Huh?" He focused on the road as he tried to decipher what his niece meant. "We all need love, sweetie." He gulped. If this was parenting, he was about to flunk. "Why do you ask?"

"'Cause I heard Penny talking to Miss Miranda an' Penny said you needed love so you'd stop hurting. I love you real lots and Kyle does, too."

"I don't think I have any special hurt today, sweetheart, but if I did, for sure your hug would fix it," he said. Penny had said he needed love? What in the world? Suddenly a lightbulb clicked on inside his head.

Could Penny be matchmaking?

Had she misunderstood their last conversation and decided that he needed a woman in his life?

Once they were home and the kids were tucked in, the idea came to him. Maybe it was Penny who needed a matchmaker.

He sat down to make a list of male friends who might fit her bill. Only thing was, he ended up deleting most of them because imagining Penny with any of his buddies gave Rick an unsettled feeling in his stomach.

Must have been the fast food. Certainly couldn't be because he was interested in Penny's personal life.

Lois Richer loves traveling, swimming and quilting, but mostly she loves writing stories that show God's boundless love for His precious children. As she says, "His love never changes or gives up. It's always waiting for me. My stories feature imperfect characters learning that love doesn't mean attaining perfection. Love is about keeping on keeping on." You can contact Lois via email, loisricher@gmail.com, or on Facebook (loisricherauthor).

Books by Lois Richer

Love Inspired

Wranglers Ranch

The Rancher's Family Wish
Her Christmas Family Wish
The Cowboy's Easter Family Wish
The Twins' Family Wish

Family Ties

A Dad for Her Twins
Rancher Daddy
Gift-Wrapped Family
Accidental Dad

Visit the Author Profile page at Harlequin.com for more titles.

The Twins' Family Wish

Lois Richer

LOVE INSPIRED BOOKS

Recycling programs
for this product may
not exist in your area.

ISBN-13: 978-0-373-62287-0

The Twins' Family Wish

www.Harlequin.com

Printed in U.S.A.

The Lord will work out His plan for your life.
—*Psalms* 138:8

To all the moms, would-be moms
and those who have a heart for mothering.

Chapter One

"Are you buying that for your little girl?"

Startled from her reverie about children and the lack of them in her life, Penelope Stern dropped the stuffed pig onto the display and wheeled around. A child with lopsided pigtails and thoughtful brown eyes studied her for a moment before picking up the animal herself to study it more closely.

"Moms always like pink," she proclaimed, her head tilted to one side. "Mine did, too." Her face got a soft, weepy look. "But I don't gots a mom no more."

"Oh?" Moved by her woeful expression and the sorrowful sound of loss in her voice, it took a minute before Penny's brain clicked in. "But I'm not a mo—"

"Katie?" The word emerged from behind Penny, a low male growl that held both reproof and resignation. "I asked you and Kyle to stay with me, remember?" The man held up a hand when Katie's bow lips parted. "And no, we can't buy that toy because you already have a zoo full of stuffed animals at home."

Penny watched as the tall, lean dad gently lifted the pig from the child's hand and returned it to the shelf.

Handsome yet disheveled in battered cowboy boots, jeans that had seen a lot of wear and a red-and-white-checked shirt that was missing two buttons, he shoved back his Stetson, tenderly brushed his hand over the child's head then looked up at Penny.

"I hope Katie wasn't bothering you."

"Oh, no, she wasn't bother—" Only the strictest control kept Penny from gasping when she glimpsed the angrily crumpled skin that scarred the left side of his very handsome face. She met his gaze and mentally winced at his expression—as if he was resigned to people staring at him, as if he was waiting for her to turn away in disgust, as if that had happened before. "Katie wasn't bothering me at all." She hoped her smile would cover her disconcerted reaction.

"She's buyin' that pig for her little girl, Uncle Rick." Katie grabbed the pig and returned it to Penny. "She'll like it," the sprite promised, pigtails bobbing. Then she leaned on Uncle Rick's arm and yawned. "Is it time to go home now? I'm tired."

"Well, darlin', I've almost finished my list but now Kyle's wandered off." The man heaved a sigh that said better than any words could that he, too, was weary and more than ready to leave. "Let's go find your brother."

"May I help you look for him?" Penny wouldn't have offered her help to a total stranger except that she'd been lost in a store once when she was four, and she hated the thought of another child going through the angst she'd suffered.

Also, although it was almost 10:00 p.m., Penny, like everyone else in Tucson, didn't relish going back out into the late June heat wave that had enveloped the city for two straight weeks. She'd only lived here about fourteen months but she'd quickly discovered that the desert's extremely high summer temperatures made shopping at night common for most Tucsonans. Added to that, her underperforming A/C made returning to her home less appealing.

"What does Kyle look like?" she asked.

"Like me. Only he gots short hair." Katie grinned at her. Then with a sudden whoop of "There he is!" went racing away from them down the bread aisle, pigtails dancing, pink sandals slapping against the tile floor, her bright pink sundress fluttering around her tanned legs.

"Thanks for the offer of help," the man said with a smile. "I think we're good now. Hope your daughter likes that." He jerked his head toward the pig she still held then quickly strode after the pair.

"I don't have a—" Penny was talking to herself. "Daughter," she finished with a grimace as she dropped the toy. When it had joined its friends, she resumed pushing her cart, which, unlike the cowboy's burgeoning one, held only two tomatoes and a head of lettuce. Thanks to the encounter with Katie and Uncle Rick, Penny shopped for the rest of the items on her list while mourning her lack of family.

When will that ache go away, Lord?

With a sigh for what couldn't be, she checked off the last item, added an impulse purchase of cashews and hazelnut coffee beans then pushed her cart to the checkout line. Since the line was long she picked up a magazine to peruse. She was studying an article about a celebrity's sixth pregnancy when she felt someone watching her.

Penny glanced over one shoulder. The same man stood in line behind her. He held the little girl in one arm, her dark head snuggled into the crook of his scarred neck as she slept, her hand squeezing the pink pig. The man's other hand guided a cart piled high with groceries. Nestled between two gallons of milk and a bag of shiny red apples, a sleeping boy sat hunched over, arms folded on the handles of the cart, his head resting on them, chubby fingers wrapped around a bright white whale.

The heart-wrenching photo moment brought tears to Penny's eyes and revived the pang of yearning she constantly fought to quell. This man had what she craved. Family. Loved ones. Somebody to cherish, to be cherished by.

Uncle Rick had what Penny constantly prayed for but had never received.

"Seems like everybody's shopping tonight, doesn't it?" he said with a friendly smile that barely moved the damaged skin on his face. "I'm Rick Granger. I guess you've already met one of my kids."

His kids? But the little girl, Katie, had called him *uncle.*

"Penny Stern," she said quickly.

"You decided not to get the pig for your daughter," he said with a glance at her cart. "Smart lady. I've been conned into buying a pig *and* a whale." His rueful smile brushed over the twins like a caress. "My only excuse is that I couldn't help it. They kind of reach in and squeeze the 'no' right out of you," he said fondly. Then he looked up. "How old is your daughter?"

"I don't have a daughter. I don't have any children. I'm not married." Penny almost groaned out loud. *Why did you have to tell him all that? Are you so desper-*

ate for a family you'll talk to any guy with kids in the grocery store?

"You don't? But I thought Katie said—" Rick stopped then shook his shaggy dark head, which Penny noted was the same color as the kids'. Her attention was snared by the rueful expression now flickering through eyes as brown as Katie's. "I should have known, I guess, because sometimes they make up stuff."

"Oh, no, Katie didn't make up anything," she assured him. "I was looking at the toys and she probably assumed—"

Startled by the cashier's loud "Next!" Penny blushed as she cut off her explanation, slid her cart to the counter and began setting her groceries on the belt.

"She assumed?" the man prompted.

"That I was a mom. I'm actually a kindergarten teacher." Why she felt compelled to explain the details of her life while her bill was tallied was a mystery to Penny. But it didn't stop her. "I like to keep abreast of the marketplace of kids' toys."

"Ah." Rick stood waiting as she paid. Suddenly realizing how much she'd talked to a man she didn't know disconcerted Penny. She felt a little nervous as she gathered up her grocery sacks. She was ready to leave when she noticed his struggle to hold Katie and unload his purchases.

"May I help you?" The offer was out of her mouth before she could stop it. When he nodded she decided she could hardly retract. Penny set down her sacks and began removing the items from his cart. Out of habit she placed them in categories; cans first, boxes next— many of which were varieties of cookies, she noted with a frown and then scolded herself for her interest.

Maybe the kids' aunt can't bake.

She arranged meat and then dairy—she had to gently shift Kyle to get the milk but thankfully he remained asleep—then added the produce and at last the cart was emptied.

"There you go."

"Thank you very much." Rick held up each child's hand with fingers still clutched around their toys so the cashier could scan them. It was only as he swiped his credit card that Penny realized she was staring and that the cashier had noticed.

"The parking lot's kind of rough." It was a lame attempt to cover her interest in the little family but some inner need to help made Penny offer, "Would you like me to steer your cart so Kyle doesn't wake up?"

Hearing the cashier's snicker made Penny wish she'd simply walked away. She must sound desperate and yet something about this little family drew her.

Rick was apparently oblivious to both the cashier's amusement and Penny's inner turmoil because all he said was "Thanks."

Penny shifted her two bags into his cart then pushed it through the automatic doors and across the heated pavement, trying to match his long strides though her wedge-heeled sandals and shorter height made that difficult. She huffed a sigh of relief when he finally stopped beside a shiny black truck.

"Well, thanks for your help," he said with a grin. "Again."

But Penny remained frozen in place, her gaze captivated by his tender expression as he slid sweet little Katie into a car seat and tenderly belted her in. When she stirred momentarily, he pressed a kiss against her brow, waited for her to settle then went through the same process with Kyle. He treated the children as if they were precious cargo, not as if he was in a hurry to get home and shove them into bed. He loved them.

"So, uh, thanks a lot for your help." Rick gave Penny a funny look when she didn't move. With a frown then a shrug he turned his back and began storing his groceries in the truck.

The sound of the truck box closing finally drew Penny out of her stupor. She blushed with embarrassment.

"Good night." She racewalked away from them to her car feeling like she'd peeked in on something private and special. Yet no matter how she tried, as she drove home to her condo she couldn't erase the image of Rick's loving glance at the children.

Why were they *his* kids, she wondered? And what would it be like to be adored like that? Questions about Rick and his darling little family tortured her all the way home until Penny told herself to stop wanting what she couldn't have.

Remember Psalm 138:8? The Lord will work out His plan for your life.

Quashing the image of Katie and Kyle and their hunky uncle, Penny reminded herself that she'd decided teaching kindergarten kids would be enough.

But her heart asked, *Will it?*

As Rick drove through the night to his ranch, he savored the peace of sleeping children while at the same time worrying about how he'd manage tomorrow. Three nannies in three weeks had to be a record, even for the twins. This was only June. With the rest of their summer vacation looming he had to find some kind of permanent caregiver for them.

There was still daycare, of course. Lots of parents enrolled their kids in summer daycare, and their children seemed to enjoy it. His business partner did that. But Rick had heard his sister, Gillian, say a thousand times that she wanted her kids to be cared for at home, by her, one-on-one. Well, Gillian wasn't here anymore, and the twins' home was his home now. But Rick couldn't stay with them full-time. He had a construction company to run.

Rick had mentioned his difficulty to his parents but they kept reassuring him that Gillian would be proud of him no matter what he did. Nice thought but it did nothing to appease the guilt nestled inside him. He was the twins' guardian because Gillian trusted him to do his best for Katie and Kyle. Good enough wasn't his best.

"This is where You step in, God," he murmured. "I need help. Now that Greg's out with that back operation I've got to keep the company running on my own. It isn't easy to keep all our jobs going, let alone make time for the kids. Can't You send someone to care for them as Gillian would have done, as a mother would?"

The company wasn't behind but there was the job at Wranglers Ranch coming up and that had Rick worried. He needed to start building those cabins immediately or he'd miss their September first completion deadline. The one thing he and Greg had vowed when they'd started RG Construction was that they'd always keep their promises. The day he'd buried his sister, Rick had promised Gillian the same.

Boy, he missed her. If only…

With a sigh for what couldn't be changed, Rick

pulled into his yard and up to the front porch, grimacing when his headlights highlighted the unfinished projects littering his yard. He'd only had the place a few months before the kids arrived, just long enough to build a basketful of dreams and fill a notebook of plans. Paint the outbuildings, repair the pasture fences, buy some horses to breed, trim the long grass and cut the overgrown bushes—that was only the beginning of what needed doing. But he hadn't started any of it because now his days were consumed with caring for Kyle and Katie, making sure they were safe and as happy as possible as they all adjusted to life without Gillian.

Actually, Rick wasn't upset by the sidelining of his plans. He'd gladly do whatever it took to keep Katie and Kyle healthy and happy. He'd vowed that six months ago, the day he'd carried them out of their burning home, the day he'd failed to save Gillian.

Caring for Gillian's kids was *his* duty and nothing would change that. Not the grief that almost consumed him every time he thought of his sister dying in that inferno. Not the urging of his former fiancée, Gina, who'd not only been repulsed by his scars but also determined not to burden her upcoming marriage with someone else's children, which had ended their relationship. Certainly not the twins' paternal grandparents, who were still deeply mourning the loss of their only son, who'd died last year on the mission field.

Rick carried the kids inside and tucked each into bed, loving their sleepy hugs and moist good-night kisses against his scarred cheek.

"Love you, Uncle Rick."

"Love you, too," he whispered, his throat closing with emotion.

Only when they were fast asleep did he retrieve the groceries from the truck. Once they were put away Rick sat on his porch, savoring the night's cooler breezes that washed down the slopes of the Rincon Mountains. He resumed his earlier prayer.

"You know I'm committed to the kids. Only how am I supposed to do my job *and* care for them, Lord?" he murmured just before thunder rumbled in the distance.

No answer. How did you make sense of God when two little kids bawled because they wanted to be held by their mommy, and you could do nothing to stop their tears?

When lightning split the sky in a brilliant spear that hurt the eyes, Rick went inside. Katie might wake up afraid or Kyle might need a drink. He had to be there for them.

"I'm hanging on to my faith by a thread here," he whispered as sheets of rain pelted the tired old ranch house. "I could use some help, something to show me that You care for us, have a plan in store for us, that something good is on the way. Please?"

He waited, not sure what he expected. But when the rain stopped and the moon came out, nothing had changed. Rick was still a single parent to two recently bereaved kids, with a major building contract scheduled to start in two days.

"Could you at least send me a nanny?" he prayed desperately. "Someone like that woman I met at the grocery store?"

Penny. Her face filled his mind—pretty, happy, fresh-faced and eager to embrace life. Her short, spiky blond hair tousled so it emphasized big blue eyes that glowed whenever she looked at the kids. She'd said she was a teacher so she'd know how to handle kids. And she was practical. Look at the way she'd organized his groceries and then pushed his cart.

"Yeah, somebody like her would be perfect. Can you send me someone like Penny? For the kids' sake?"

It was a desperation prayer, unworthy of the faith his parents had instilled in him since he was Kyle's age. But since this plea was for the twins' sake Rick didn't mind asking for the impossible.

He wasn't sure what he expected but when nothing happened he rose with a weary sigh, prepared the breakfast bar for the morning meal and set the coffeepot to start automatically.

Then Rick dropped into bed and fell asleep to the memory of Penny's musical voice saying, "Let me help you."

Chapter Two

"Do you think Wranglers Ranch Day Care has enough toys?"

Startled, Penny whirled around. Rick Granger stood in the doorway, a twin on either side. The three of them gaped in disbelief at the big room bulging with every conceivable plaything a child could dream of.

"Please come in." Penny chuckled at the astonished expressions. "Almost enough," she teased.

"Almost? You couldn't get any more toys onto those shelves," Rick said with a shake of his head.

"You might be surprised. Hi, Katie. I love your dress." Penny hid her shock at seeing Katie's shorn hair stuck up in odd places and managed to return the little girl's grin before turning to her brother. "And you're Kyle. I don't believe we've met. I'm Penny." She smiled at him. "Would you two like to play with the blocks on that table while your uncle and I have a chat?"

One glance at the toys and the kids took off, leaving Rick and Penny alone.

"The toys are Sophie's fault," Penny explained with a laugh. Then she frowned. "You know Sophie, right?"

"Sophie Johns, wife of Tanner, owners of Wranglers Ranch." Rick nodded. "Tanner is a good friend of mine, and now he's also a client."

"Okay, good. So anyway, Sophie said that buying so much helped her convince herself that her dream was actually going to happen." Penny glanced around, pleased with what they'd accomplished. "She's dreamed of starting an on-site daycare for Wranglers employees since baby Carter was born." She noted his wide-eyed look and tongue in cheek asked, "Is it too much?"

"For anyone else, maybe." Rick looked at her with a straight face but his dark eyes were twinkling. "In Sophie's case, it's probably restrained."

"You *do* know her." Penny burst out laughing.

"She said you wanted to talk to me." He checked his watch as if he had a hundred things to do and was mentally preparing to tick this one off his list.

"Yes, I do. I'd tell you to have a seat but—" Embarrassed, she swallowed the rest of her comment.

"I wouldn't fit?" Rick's brown eyes crinkled at the corners with his grin. "No, I wouldn't. So I'll sit here." He sank onto the floor and crossed his legs in front of him, one knee poking through the rip in his jeans. He set his Stetson beside him then smiled at her. "Nice to see you again, Penny."

"You, too, Rick." Penny cleared her throat and assumed her most businesslike tone, refusing to let her gaze stray to the scar on his cheek. "Sophie asked if I might be able to help you with caring for the twins until Wranglers Ranch Day Care opens. Then she said that they will attend here."

"That's what she told me, too." Rick blinked at her

in surprise before he glanced around once more. "She also said this place will open July first."

"That's the goal." Penny arched one eyebrow. "So before I know if I can help you I'd like to know about a regular day in your life and what you need for the twins."

"Sorry if I look a little surprised. I had no idea Sophie was going to ask you to help." He frowned then swallowed. "So my partner and I own a construction company. Since he's out with medical issues, I've had to take on running all three of our crews. I don't want to lay off any of my men but the pace of running so many jobs on my own is hectic." Rick stole a quick glance at the giggling twins. "Six months ago the twins lost their mother, my sister, G-Gillian, in a house fire."

"Oh, no." Her heart crimped with sympathy when he stumbled over her name. "I'm so sorry."

"Thanks." Rick paused then continued in a stronger tone. "I'm the twins' guardian so I need to do everything I can to provide them with a good home, which I'm trying to do. But I can't be with them all the time. Even though I want to."

"Of course you can't, but good for you for wanting to," she said and meant it.

"So I need some help. The thing is—" Rick cleared his throat then looked directly at her "—I'm not very knowledgeable about the whole fatherhood thing but I feel like the twins need stability and I don't feel I'm providing that because my hours are so long. Most daycare hours don't coordinate with my schedule, and nannies—well, let's say they haven't worked that well for us." He lowered his gaze to his hands. "The twins are a bit—" He paused, obviously searching for the right descriptive.

"Mischievous?" Penny supplied and chuckled when he nodded, his look dour.

"Exactly. I hired a very experienced woman named Helga to watch them. One day when she fell asleep Katie tied her shoelaces together. In knots. Helga quit." He sighed as if her resignation had been unpleasant. "Next I hired a younger person to work with the kids, a guy who had a lot of energy and a list of impressive credentials. He kept the twins busy but he had some, er, unusual ideas about the kind of stories they needed to fuel their imaginations. His vampire tales caused the kids some sleepless nights and neither they nor I could handle all his zombie talk."

"Oh, dear." Rick's fed-up expression forced Penny to stifle her amusement.

"Someone suggested I try a student who was looking for a summer job so I hired my neighbor's daughter to babysit."

"That sounds like a good idea," Penny murmured encouragingly.

"It should have been but she got a little too busy texting her boyfriend and let Katie and Kyle make lunch. My insurance company dropped me after that fiasco and I dropped her." Rick threw up his hands. "Have I scared you off yet?"

"No. Children need to be kept busy and they require close supervision." Penny glanced at the twins, trying not to stare at Katie's almost bald spot. Poor little orphans. "So basically you require someone to care for them while you work."

"Yes. But everyone I've talked to wants a set schedule and I can't offer that. If something at a job comes up, I have to be there." He looked—embarrassed? "But that's not all."

"It's not?" Intrigued, Penny waited.

"Actually, my problem is twofold. *I'm* struggling with leaving the twins with others." He looked ashamed by the admission and also stubborn, both at the same time. "Katie and Kyle just lost their mother. I want them to feel secure. But whenever I picked them up from daycare, they seemed sad. That's why I thought having somebody come to my place would be easier for them and maintain some stability in their world."

"But it also makes finding care more challenging," she guessed.

"I know." Rick sighed. "The kids talk about how much they miss Gillian. That's natural and they don't do it constantly. But those moments aren't scripted. They just happen. So I can't ask them to wait until seven each night or Saturday morning to talk about it. If I'm not there for them when they need me—" His gloomy face revealed how deeply he was torn by the situation. "I'm trying to do my best but sometimes they cry. A lot. I must be doing something wrong."

"That's not necessarily true, Rick." Penny's heart went out to him. This man was so determined to do the right thing for two bereaved little kids. She admired him very much.

"What do you mean?" Was that hope brightening his dark eyes?

"Being together without Gillian is a time of change for all of you. You're all in mourning for someone you loved a great deal. Kids often express their feelings by crying." She smiled at him. "Don't worry. Those sharing moments will still happen. Katie and Kyle will still turn to you when they need you." She glanced over one shoulder, noting how well adjusted the twins seemed. "You know there's nothing wrong with choosing part-time daycare and part-time one-on-one care. Whatever works best for you should drive your decision. That and the twins' welfare."

"Are you sure?" He looked relieved when she nodded.

"Positive. To me, Katie and Kyle seem very well adjusted though I haven't known them long. As long as they know you'll be there if they need you, I think you'll see that they will feel secure." Privately Penny wondered if Rick ever took any time for himself but decided now wasn't the time to ask.

"So would you be able to care for them? I know that as a teacher you're around kids all the time and this is your break time—" He stopped when she shook her head.

"Not quite. At school I have children around me for about six hours." Penny glanced at the twins, smiling at the massive tower they'd built. "Teachers are free at recess and lunch hour. Also, I don't wake up with children or take them home with me at the end of my day as you do."

Though I wish I could.

"You're saying teaching isn't like parenting. Okay, I get that." But Rick still didn't look convinced.

"If I asked, I suspect you'd say building is your passion. Well, kids are mine." Penny held his gaze as she made her point. "As a teacher, I want the kids I work with to learn strength and self-reliance. I want them to grow into positive adults with the skills that will help them learn how to manage their world."

"Admirable," he agreed with a nod. "But it seems like that's a lot to ask of a teacher in a public school situation."

"Believe me, in these hard economic times with all the strife in our country, that is something I struggle with every day I teach—to make time for the important stuff." Penny smiled. "But this is about you, Rick. And the twins. So tell me a little more about your lives."

"Okay. Gillian and her husband were missionaries in Mali, West Africa. A little over a year ago he died there in an uprising. She was bereft and moved home with the twins. And then Gillian died—" He stopped. Gulped and started again. "The twins have had it very rough. I'm trying to make up for their loss."

"You can't, Rick." It was hard to say but this man needed to hear the truth so in spite of his pinched lips Penny kept going. "It doesn't matter what you say or how much you do. You will never be able to replace Katie and Kyle's parents."

"But—" The poor man looked so devastated that Penny wanted to hug him. Instead she rushed to reassure him.

"What you *can* do is be the very best uncle you're able. That's what they most need right now," she added.

Just then Katie walked over and snuggled under his arm. Rick smiled at her, brushed a kiss against the top of her shorn head and hugged her close. Thus reassured, Katie skipped back to where her brother played.

"See? You were just there for Katie. That's what they need." Penny couldn't stifle her curiosity about this man and his family. "Do they have grandparents?"

"Two sets. Their dad's parents live in New Hampshire. They're still devastated by their son's death, and ill health makes it tough for them to visit Tucson so I set it up for the kids to Skype with them once a week." Rick gazed at her as if to ask if he was doing the right thing.

"That's very smart of you. Keeping family close to us helps lessen a loss." Or so the books said. Penny didn't have any family so she had no firsthand experience, but it seemed logical. She waited but when he didn't say anything more, she asked, "And your parents?"

"They live near Sonoita, which isn't that far from Tucson, but they're kept really busy during summer with the lake, their motel and a restaurant so they don't come here often. I try to run the twins down as often as I can." Rick stared at the pair with stark grief on his face. "I think it helps ease Mom and Dad's loss over Gillian when they're with the twins."

"I'm sure. Who helps ease your loss?" The moment the question left her lips, Penny regretted asking it. She sounded nosy.

"You're asking about a wife or a girlfriend?" He shook his dark head. "I was engaged but Gina called it off after the accident. Turns out she didn't want a marriage with two kids in the mix, which was a good thing to learn then because there was no way I would ever abandon my sister's children. Not after I—"

I what? she wanted to demand, frustrated that he left the words hanging.

Penny waited for Rick to pull himself out of the introspection he'd fallen in. She truly admired his sturdy love and commitment for the two orphaned children. Liked his tough determination to do the best for them. He was kind, generous and sincere. Best of all, he was one of those men who paid attention to the most important things in life—like family.

Penny knew that if she took on the twins she'd enjoy friendship with Rick, too, but she'd have to get rid of that flutter of appreciation that winked inside her when he looked at her. He was extremely good-looking despite the scar and he had a warm, engaging personality.

But Penny had allowed herself to fall in love twice and both times it had backfired, leaving her decimated and filled with crippling self-worth. She was better now, more in control. Enough so that she had vowed she would never again depend on any man to fulfill her dreams or to create her happily-ever-after. Instead she was going to focus on making her dreams come true on her own.

Well, with God's help.

Romance? Well, *if* it came along sometime in the future, she'd consider it. But she wasn't going to look for love. Love was something for the future. Maybe. Not now. Not even if Rick Granger made her heart pitter-patter and her stomach beat in time to a Sousa march.

Penny had survived the worst. Now she was looking for the best God had to offer. Getting dumped when her world was falling apart had taught her self-reliance.

Despite this hunky uncle and his adorable twins, she wasn't going to risk heartache again.

"Does teaching help you know so much about kids?" Rick asked, glancing at Penny's bare ring finger. "Because you said you don't have your own kids."

"I guess." She pinched her lips together but when he raised an eyebrow she explained in a tight, strained voice. "I'm neither married nor a mom."

"Seems like a mistake on some man's part." He shrugged at her surprised look. "You're beautiful and smart and educated."

"Well, thank you. I think." The perky smile Penny usually wore disappeared, leaving her looking like a wounded bird, ducking her head against her chest as if she was uncomfortable.

Funny. Rick barely knew her and yet he couldn't imagine Penny without children around her. She'd been so good with Katie that night at the store.

"You don't want a family?"

"It's impossible." Clearly she did not want to talk about it. "To get back to babysitting the twins. As you know, I'm helping Sophie organize Wranglers Ranch Day Care. That means that when it's up and running you'll be able to bring Katie and Kyle here while you're working on-site building the cabins, right?"

"That's what she said. But what about until then? And when I finish the job here, what do I do? The twins will still need someone to care for them on the days they don't attend school." Stymied and eager for her advice, Rick was pretty sure getting to know this lady would be very interesting.

"I can help you out occasionally," Penny offered. "And I might know an older lady who could alternate with me, if needed." Her eyes were once more that desert-sky blue, rich and fathomless. Penny Stern might look frail and delicate with those silvery-blond wisps framing her gamine face, but Rick had a hunch that this woman had the courageous heart of a lioness. "Would that work?"

"Yes, but what about you?" Rick studied her. "Summer is your vacation. Don't you have plans?"

"Not really. I was going to go water-skiing with my friend and her husband. That's my most favorite thing to do. But they're using their summer break to tour Australia." Penny shrugged as if it didn't matter. "I'll probably head to the beach for a weekend here and there, do some painting at my house, volunteer for Vacation Bible School at church in August. Stuff like that." She grinned. "*And* watch Katie and Kyle."

It sounded boring and the very last thing Rick would have thought about Penny Stern was that she lived a boring life.

"Are you sure you want to do this?" When she nodded, he told her as much as he could about his schedule, emphasizing that he often had to change the times when he picked up the twins. "I need to keep all my men working so I'm back and forth between sites a lot, troubleshooting and fixing issues that come up, sometimes at odd hours."

"Must be demanding." She studied him then glanced at the clock on the wall. "What about now? Do you have today off?"

"I wish." He barked a laugh. "I've got to be on-site to pour a foundation in half an hour. The agency couldn't find a sitter on such short notice so I guess the twins will just have to come along."

Rick hated doing that because it would be so dull for them. Construction job sites were just about the worst place for kids, but after yesterday afternoon's fiasco when the temporary sitter had lost Katie at the park for over two hours before calling him, he had no choice. He wouldn't leave them with her again.

"Um, can I ask what happened to Katie's pigtails?"

Penny murmured, studying the back of the little girl's head with a frown.

So much for being a capable parent.

"She cut them off." Rick squirmed, knowing Penny would bawl him out for his carelessness.

"She got hold of scissors?" There was nothing in Penny's voice that accused him but Rick felt guilty all the same.

"My electric razor. Last night." He heaved a sigh. "I thought they were asleep. I should have been doing books but I conked out. Something woke me up. Katie was in the bathroom, half-shorn, and most of her hair was in the sink. Kyle had dared her and Katie never refuses a dare." He raked a frustrated hand through his hair when his phone made a noise. "Excuse me." He scanned the text then quickly rose. "I need to go. When would you be able to care for the kids?"

"I could start now." Penny also rose and smiled at him. "Are you sure you trust me, Rick?"

"You come highly recommended by Tanner and Sophie. I trust them implicitly." He made a face. "Anyway, I doubt you can do worse at childcare than me."

"Given the state of Katie's hair that's not exactly a vote of confidence," she teased then shrugged. "Don't beat yourself up, Rick. She didn't get hurt and hair grows back. Kids do things that are utterly unpredictable."

"Not to you, I'll wager." He watched her face, saw distaste in the way she wrinkled her pert nose.

"You think?" Penny gave a half laugh and shook her head. "A student once brought a snake to school in his backpack. He hadn't told his parents he'd found it. A python. He put it in my desk." She nodded at his disbelief. "True story."

Rick liked the way her eyes sparkled with amusement. Penny didn't take her world too seriously it seemed. "What did you do?"

"I prayed. Really, really hard. Then closed the drawer and called the janitor." She smiled. "So you fell asleep last night. You were tired and who wouldn't be? Caring for one child is taxing. You have two to watch over and you're not used to doing it."

He opened his mouth to protest but Penny held up a hand.

"It will get easier, I promise. Why don't you take today off as a caregiver, focus on work and leave the kids with me? I'll take Katie to get a haircut, if that's okay with you?" Penny waited until he nodded.

Rick was happy to turn that task over to her. He figured she'd know more than he did about little girls' hairstyles.

"After a trim we'll think of something fun we can do for the rest of the day." She did not seem fazed by the prospect. "Do they have allergies to anything?"

"No." Rick wanted so badly to accept but something inside him hesitated. *What if—*

"It's really okay, Uncle Rick." Penny didn't sound irritated by his indecision. "I won't let anything happen to them. I promise." She wrote on a piece of paper then held it out. "My cell phone number."

"Thank you." *This is an answer to prayer, stupid. Take it!* "Here's mine." He waited till she'd written it down then called, "Katie and Kyle, can you come here for a moment?"

Rick carefully explained to the twins that they were

going to stay with Penny for a while. Katie's lip trembled for about a nanosecond, until Penny mentioned a water park. Both kids whooped for joy.

"But their swimsuits—I didn't bring them." Rick frowned at her.

"I'll handle it." What assurance those words held.

He had to ask. "Are you sure?"

"Positive. We're going to have so much fun." Penny's face glowed when she smiled and suddenly any reservation he felt was gone. "Call me to pick them up whenever you're ready. We'll be fine. Guys, let's go get your car seats and say goodbye to Uncle Rick."

A second summons from his phone forced Rick to leave more quickly than he wanted but as he drove away, he saw Penny pushing a laughing Katie on a swing in the yard outside the daycare building while Kyle whooped as he raced down a slide.

Rick smiled as he waved but his thoughts were on the past. If only he hadn't let Gillian die. If only he'd run faster, forced himself through that choking blanket of smoke a second time, pushed through the searing pain of those burning embers on his face to get to her. Maybe, just maybe—

With a sigh of resignation Rick headed toward the job site. Recriminations didn't help. Somehow he'd have to readjust his focus on the present and not the past so the twins didn't suffer.

At least he had Penny's help. For now.

Rick liked the pretty woman a lot, liked her spirit and unstinting kindness. Liked the fearlessness in her face when she broached a subject. But liking was all he would allow. He had to concentrate his entire focus on the kids, on making their world as happy as Gillian would have. It didn't matter what he gave up. It was all about them and that meant he had no time for romance. Rick would have gladly sacrificed a lot more than that if he could have his sister back.

Since he couldn't he would spend every day making the world the best it could be for Katie and Kyle and he'd take Penny's help every time she offered. Help and friendship, yes.

Anything more wasn't possible.

Chapter Three

Hungry, dirty and very weary by the time he arrived at Penny's that evening, Rick paused a moment to survey her home. The lovely adobe structure in the old Southwest style had a rose trellis climbing up the outside walls and a towering saguaro cactus that shielded the front windows from the heat of the desert sun.

Though he didn't yet know Penny well, he thought the house suited her. It was warm and inviting just like she was. Maybe sometime down the road he could ask her for hints on how to make his ranch as hospitable.

Keep focused on today.

"Come on in, Rick," Penny invited in a friendly though hushed voice. "The twins are asleep. I'm afraid I wore them out."

"Great. Then they should sleep well tonight." And maybe without a nightmare. "I'll get their car seats then load them up so we can get out of your hair," he said, admiring the homeyness she'd created inside. This was a place where a family could relax and enjoy each other; you could see the hospitality in the warm colors and soft welcoming furniture. So why did Penny always seem to be alone? "I'm sorry it took me so long."

"No problem. I'm having cookies and lemonade. Want to join me?" Wearing a sleeveless bright yellow top and white shorts, Penny's bare feet and tousled blond hair made her look cool and comfortable, a far cry from the worn-out caregiver he'd expected to find. "The twins helped me bake the cookies so you have to try some."

"Uh—okay." Like it was a hardship. Rick was starving. "I hope you didn't have any trouble getting them to eat supper? They're picky eaters, I know."

"I roasted a chicken with some new potatoes and spring vegetables. They seemed to enjoy it." Penny frowned at him, making Rick wonder if his tongue was hanging out at the sound of roast chicken. "Did *you* eat dinner?"

"No time to eat today. It was crazy busy. I'll get something when I get the twins to bed." He said it quickly with a shrug, downplaying it so he wouldn't look like he was asking Penny to feed him. No way did he want to impose on this woman's generosity. Caring for the twins for an entire day was far more than he'd dared to hope for.

"There are plenty of leftovers, Rick. I'll heat a plate for you." Before he could object Penny had opened the fridge and was pulling out containers. "I always make way too much," she said when she noticed his surprise at the amount of food she was removing. Her cheeks pinked, enhancing her blue eyes. "Roast chicken is my favorite meal. It always makes me think of family dinners and…"

Her voice trailed away as she turned, set the filled plate in the microwave and started it.

"Do you have a big family?" Penny's comments gave Rick an opportunity to satisfy his curiosity about her.

"Actually, I'm an orphan." She looked a little wistful as she explained. "Apparently I was about two days old when I was found on some church steps in Seattle. I've never discovered who left me there or why. But I used to imagine—" She stopped, swallowed then focused on him. "Anyway, my childhood was nothing like yours."

"Mine?" He frowned. "How did you—?"

"The twins, of course." She grinned at him. "They said you and their mother grew up with your family beside a lake here in Arizona." Penny shook her head. "How blessed were you?"

"Very blessed," he agreed. "I had a great childhood." He watched as she poured a big glass of lemonade and set it in front of him. Cookies sat piled high on a platter in the middle of the table. "Chocolate chip?" He was surprised when she shook her head.

"As a treat for sitting so still while we had Katie's hair cut, I bought the twins ice cream cones at the water park. I thought it would be wise to tone down the rest of the sugar content today so these are coconut oatmeal with a bit of honey as a sweetener. Try one," she invited, then as the microwave beeped revised, "Or maybe after you eat dinner."

Penny's roast chicken dinner was delicious. Rick savored every bite of his abundant serving then finished it off with a third glass of lemonade.

"This is really delicious," he said, savoring the tangy flavor. "What kind is it?"

"Uh, lemonade." Penny looked confused by the question.

"I meant what brand." When she frowned he immediately realized his mistake. "This isn't from a package, or frozen, is it?" When she shook her head, Rick noticed the bits of lemon floating among the chunks of ice and a couple of seeds that must have slipped in. "I haven't had real lemonade since I don't know when. It's very good. Did the kids drink it?"

"Of course." She frowned. "Why wouldn't they? They helped make it."

"Katie and Kyle made and drank real lemonade?" Rick couldn't wrap his mind around it. "You must be Wonder Woman."

"Hardly." Penny's lilting laughter filled the room but it was her face that held his attention. Though her eyes sparkled with fun, behind that he saw a steely willpower. "I offered them two choices, lemonade or water. They drank both but seemed to prefer the lemonade."

"Huh. Seems like I'm always buying juice for them, even though I know it's full of sugar." As usual, guilt rushed in. "Gillian made her own juice," he mumbled, feeling inadequate.

"Rick, you can't do everything she did," Penny said in a quiet voice. "And I doubt she'd expect you to."

Funny that he'd never considered Gillian's expectations of him.

"The twins shared some of their memories after we had dinner tonight. I know that Gillian was a great mom." Her smile altered; she grew more serious. "The thing is, Rick, a great mom has just one desire for her kids, one thing she wants above all else."

"Which is?" He waited, his interest in her opinion growing.

"A mom who truly loves her kids wants the person who cares for them when she can't to love them as much as she would. Just like you do." Penny's kind words soothed and comforted him. "I can tell that you love Katie and Kyle very much. You're doing exactly what Gillian would have wanted."

"Except it's not enough." As soon as he said it Rick wished he hadn't.

He was so tired, worn out with trying to be all things for his business, the twins and his overworked parents. He hadn't been able to get out to the lake and help them begin the summer season, as he usually did. Greg's illness meant he hadn't been able to spend as much time with his parents, helping them deal with Gillian's death. Neither had he been able to get the twins out to the lake as frequently as he should have so his grieving parents could find some solace in their daughter's children.

The truth was Rick was barely managing to juggle all the balls in his life. He spent his day moving from worksite to worksite, always dreading that he might mess up something important and make things worse. And while he kept that tucked inside, he also fought his growing fears that he'd fail to live up to what his sister wanted, that he wouldn't be there when the twins needed him, that the twins would suffer because of him.

Suddenly the weight of it all multiplied, stretching his nerves taut until he blurted, "I can't make up for it."

"For what?" Penny frowned, which puckered her smooth brow. She leaned forward to peer into his face. "What are you trying to make up for, Rick?"

He held his breath, waiting, hoping she'd let him off the hook, wouldn't force him to answer. He hadn't said this to anyone else, especially not his parents, certainly not his clients, not even to Tanner even though he was a good friend.

But Penny waited, her question hanging, begging an answer.

"Never mind." He took another cookie and chewed it so he couldn't say any more.

"I can tell that whatever has you feeling guilty is wearing you down," she guessed, her head tipped slightly to one side. "You need to let it go."

"It's not that easy." Oh, how he wished it was.

"Of course it isn't easy. The important things never are." Penny tilted her head to one side as she studied him. "I'm guessing your guilt has to do with your sister's death."

Rick remained silent while wishing he'd never brought up the subject.

"Guilt will drain you, sap your energy and change your focus. You can't dwell on it." Her soft voice was like a balm, soft and soothing.

"I can't help it." Rick raked a hand through his hair feeling as helpless as a kitten to battle the negatives that plagued him.

"But you have to for the twins' sake. They need your full attention. So does your work." Though Penny's tone remained mild she didn't mince words. "There's no room for guilt."

What would she say if she knew *why* he felt guilty, Rick wondered? Would she walk away? Would she refuse to have anything to do with him or the twins? Would she blame him?

More to the point, why did Penny's good opinion of him matter so much?

"Talk to me, Rick," she murmured.

"I tried to get Gillian out." It was like a dam breaking and once started, he couldn't stop. "I managed to fight through the flames to the twins' bedroom and carry them out of the house but when I went back in I couldn't find Gillian. The smoke was so thick you couldn't breathe. But I kept going anyway. I couldn't leave her there, alone."

"Of course you couldn't. And then?" she nudged.

"Then a burning timber fell on me and—I don't remember much more." Except the pain. He remembered that very clearly. In fact, the horror of those moments haunted him almost every night.

"It's over, Rick." Penny's soft reassurance penetrated his thoughts. "Gillian doesn't blame you."

"Doesn't she?" She should. He'd made her children orphans.

"Gillian knows that God is in control, that He will love and care for the twins better than she ever could. And she knows there was a reason for her death." Penny sounded so confident.

Rick wanted to believe her, to trust that Gillian would absolve him for his failure to save her. But even if *she* could, *he* couldn't. There was no forgiveness for letting his sister die.

"I can't accept that."

From Penny's silence and her bent head, Rick figured he'd shocked her. He rose with a silent sigh. The constant guilt he lived with every time he glanced at the twins or heard his sister's name was his punishment and he didn't begrudge it. He deserved it. But for the twins' sake he needed to keep caring for them. He didn't need more problems so why didn't God—?

"I'm sorry, Penny. I shouldn't have dumped all over you. If you can show me where the car seats are, I'll get going." Rick no longer wanted to share his aching, wretched soul, especially not with this woman, who seemed so smart and cool with her world put nicely together. "Thank you for today. We appreciate it."

Penny said nothing as she rose. She silently led him to the garage to get the two car seats from her car and carried one out to his truck. Then she led the way inside the house to her spare room, where the twins lay curled under a lovely turquoise afghan.

"I'll take Katie, you take Kyle," she whispered and tenderly lifted the little girl.

Rick followed, cradling Kyle. When the twins were safely belted in his truck, he thanked her once more.

"You went above and beyond for us. Katie's short hair looks really cute. Thank you." He handed her some bills. "I appreciate everything you've done."

"So when will you bring them tomorrow?" she asked before he could swing into his truck's driver's seat.

"When—?" Surprised, Rick frowned at her. After his pathetic confession he'd been certain her help was a onetime thing.

"Yes. When?" She arched one perfect eyebrow. "I like to be prepared."

"You're involved in getting Wranglers Ranch Day Care up and running. That's a lot of work. I appreciate your help today," he continued, "but I'm sure you don't want to spend your free time watching my kids, though it's very kind of you to offer."

Penny studied him as if she couldn't quite decide whether or not to tell him what she was thinking. After a moment she nodded.

"I told you, I love kids, Rick. All kids. Every chance I get to enjoy them is a blessing. That's why I became a teacher." He couldn't get over how that gorgeous smile of hers lit up her entire face. "It's true. I am helping Sophie organize the daycare. But I'm able to do that *and* care for the twins, if you'll allow me. The decision is yours."

Her generosity floored him. He wanted to accept so badly. It would be so nice to have help with the twins, just for a while.

"However, I have one condition," Penny added very softly, her gaze fixed on him with an intensity that was hard to ignore.

"What's that?" Why was he suddenly filled with uncertainty? Rick wondered.

"My condition is that you don't talk about guilt over Gillian's death when the twins can overhear." Her expression grew serious. "I know her loss is something you have to work out for yourself and that you're struggling with her death. I'd love to listen to your memories of Gillian. But guilt carries negativity and I don't want that to touch the twins and maybe somehow spoil their memories of their mother."

"Makes sense." Rick thought about it for several minutes. "Okay but are you sure you can handle them and the daycare and whatever else is on your plate?"

"Yes." Penny nodded, her confidence unshakable. "You can trust me."

Funny but somehow he already knew that. His heart felt light as he asked, "Is seven thirty too early?"

"No." Penny chuckled and shook her head, the strands of her moonlight-kissed hair moving in the evening breeze. "I'm usually up at five thirty so I'll have breakfast ready for all of you."

Breakfast, too? Meeting Penny was a godsend. Anticipation fluttered to life as he hoped she wasn't talking about cereal. "Thank you very much but you don't have to make us breakfast. We usually have toast and peanut butter."

"Tomorrow morning we'll have something different. And it's me who should thank you for adding some fun to my summer." The sincerity in her response could not be faked. "I truly enjoyed today with the twins. Good night, Rick."

"Good night, Penny."

As he drove away, he couldn't expunge the memory of that joyful glow in her eyes. Unlike his former fiancée, Penny *wanted* the twins, total strangers, in her life. She was excited by the prospect. He barely knew her and yet Rick could see that Penny had what his mom called "a spirit of giving." She'd certainly made his life easier.

A flicker of interest flamed inside. Underneath that fantastic smile, who was Penny Stern and why didn't she have her own kids?

If she kept on caring for the twins maybe he'd be able to figure that out.

"Thanks, God." Rick's heart overflowed with joy and relief and thanksgiving as he drove home.

Just for tonight he was going to forget about tomorrow and the day after, forget the ranch chores that needed doing and the responsibilities to his parents, to the twins and to the company that felt heavier each time he woke up.

Just for tonight he was going to relax and enjoy the gift of a blessing named Penny.

"Thanks a lot for letting the twins visit with your kids for a while." Penny savored the aroma of cinnamon as she stepped inside Sophie's kitchen. "I managed to get through all the interviews you asked me to complete."

"So you found a director for the daycare?" Sophie asked eagerly.

"Well, no. But Tanner approved my other staff selections though we'll wait for the police checks before offering employment." She accepted the large glass of iced tea and a plate bearing two fluffy golden pastries. "What do you call these?"

"Cinnamon twists. The youth group from church is coming out tonight. I thought those would go well with their campfire." Sophie exchanged pans in the oven then sat down. "Finding a director for our daycare seems to be problematic."

"There weren't a lot of applications for that position in the first place." Penny bit into the pastry and rolled her eyes. "Every time I come to Wranglers you feed me. If this keeps up I'm going to gain a lot of weight."

"Not with your schedule. The twins said you made them a full breakfast—*really early* to quote Katie. And sent a lunch with Rick." A funny smile played across Sophie's lips.

"I roasted a chicken last night. There was so much meat left that sharing it seemed smart." Penny sipped her coffee to avoid Sophie's knowing look. "I think Rick missed both lunch and supper yesterday. I thought that if he had a sandwich today, he could eat at the site without stopping to get a bite. Did the twins tell you we also packed a picnic?"

"Uh-huh. *And* watered the flowers, put out the garbage, went to the park and played catch," she said, chuckling as she ticked off each item on her fingertips. "By the time they get home tonight they'll fall into bed."

"That's the plan." Penny felt like she had to say something to erase that meaningful look on Sophie's face. "I haven't spent much time with kids outside my classroom so I'm really enjoying my interactions with the twins."

"And with Rick?" Sophie arched an eyebrow.

"I think he might become a good friend." Penny could see this friend wasn't going to accept that. "I'm not looking for anything more, Sophie. Our Bible study is teaching me that I have to live my life strong, depending on God. I have to be content with who I am as God's child and not count on other things or people to make me happy."

"Meaning no men in your life?" Sophie asked with a frown. "And no children?"

"I'm beginning to believe that not having a family is His will," Penny admitted. *Please don't ask that of me, God.*

"But you're so good with kids. You could adopt," Sophie suggested.

"I could. But is being raised by a single mom the best choice for a child? Could I handle it? Is that God's plan for me?" Penny sighed.

"Why a single mom? Don't you want to get married?" Sophie said with a frown.

"If that's God's plan. But I refuse to get fixated on some unattainable fairy tale of happily-ever-after."

"I'm a living testament that happily-ever-after happens." Her friend grinned as the door opened. "And here's my hero now. Hi, honey."

Tanner and Rick entered the kitchen.

"We're looking for a drink and something to eat in a cool place," Tanner explained after he'd kissed his wife's cheek. "We're starving."

"Tell me something I haven't heard before." Sophie set a pitcher of iced tea and a platter of baked goods on the table. "This should help."

"I didn't think you'd be working here today. I thought you said something about a foundation this morning." As Rick munched his pastry Penny thought how handsome he was then idly wondered why he hadn't had plastic surgery to repair the scar on his face.

"We went as far as we could on that job so I brought the crew over to Wranglers Ranch to work on the foundation for the second cabin. I've got to meet my deadline of finishing all of them on time or Tanner will give me grief." He pretended to wince at Tanner's nod then glanced around. "I can hear the twins but I can't see them."

"They're playing in the back room." Sophie smiled. "It's too hot for them to do much outside, but they enjoy racing around in here where it's cool."

"Wish I was a kid." Rick sipped more of his tea.

"Penny, I was thinking about those applicants we interviewed," Tanner mused. "And that we still don't have anyone to act as our daycare manager. Do you think we should run another ad?"

"Actually, I was going to suggest it." Penny frowned. "The daycare can't open without someone who's in charge."

"You'd be amazing at that job." Rick smiled at her start of surprise. "I know. You already have a career you love. I was just thinking about how good you are with the twins and I got this mental image of you with a whole bunch of kids around you and…it's silly." He gulped then concentrated on his glass of tea. "Sorry."

"Don't be sorry, Rick, because it's not silly at all." Sophie sat up straight, her eyes sparkling with excitement. "Penny would be perfect. She's already designed a program for us. She certainly has knowledge and experience and she's also chosen all of our staff—well, except for the manager."

She flopped back against her chair, her excitement waning as her husband reminded, "Honey, Penny already has a job."

"Well, yeah. There's that." Sophie's sigh made Penny laugh.

"Don't worry. We'll find a manager," she said more confidently than she felt.

"In time for our July first opening?" Sophie wondered aloud.

"I hope so." Penny smiled brightly. "We'll ask God to send someone."

Rick's brown eyes rested on her appraisingly. "Maybe He already did."

Penny lifted her head to frown at him, slightly unnerved when he winked at her. He finished his tea then rose.

"I've got to get back to work. That was delicious. Thank you," he said to Sophie. His gaze returned to Penny. "I'll pick up the kids later."

"Uh-huh." The response was automatic. As Penny watched him stride out the door and across the yard she wondered why he'd said what he had about her as manager.

"I need to prepare for that youth group that's coming tonight." Tanner kissed Sophie, waved a hand at Penny then brushed his knuckles against baby Carter's cheek, who responded with kicks and gurgles in his playpen. "Be a good boy for Mommy."

He left while Penny was lost in thought. She'd come to Tucson a little over a year ago to make a new start. Was it silly to think about changing her career focus, too?

The question preoccupied her for the rest of the day.

I could do it, she thought to herself later that night after the twins had left with Rick. *But should I?*

She sat in her garden with a cup of peppermint tea while one by one her brain listed the potential benefits of running the daycare. In spite of her determination to remain unemotional, excitement built as the idea grew.

I haven't signed my new contract with the school district yet so there wouldn't be a penalty for breaking it.

I could be around younger kids, maybe even babies like Sophie's Carter.

I could set my own curriculum, teach the things so many of my kindergarten kids had never learned like kindness and sharing, generosity and forgiveness. I could use Bible stories to give them a basic knowledge of God.

I'd see Rick every day while he's working at the ranch.

Penny resolutely squashed the last thought and brought her focus back to job possibilities.

Wranglers Ranch was all about reaching kids for God through many outreach programs, most using some form of horsemanship. Tanner and Sophie had made it a place where kids could come, feel safe and be heard. Why couldn't she be part of that by helping to reach the very youngest kids in a way that teaching in a public school could never allow?

The more Penny thought about it, the more attractive the idea became.

But was this what God wanted for her? How could she know for sure?

"I'll post another ad for the daycare manager," she murmured, staring up at the starry heavens. "Then if You send someone better suited for the job, I'll know it's not Your will for me."

But oh, how she wanted it. Pouring herself into kids' lives, spending as many hours as she wanted with them at Wranglers Ranch, unlike at school when the kids went home to their families midafternoon or took three months off for holidays and left her with an empty classroom—surely running the daycare meant she'd never be alone again unless she wanted to be. Kind of like Rick wasn't alone.

Now why did her thoughts keep drifting back to him?

Chapter Four

"**Y**ou resigned your teaching job?" Three days later Rick sagged against the door frame at Wranglers Ranch Day Care as he stared at Penny in disbelief. "Was that wise?"

"Why? You don't think I'm capable of running a daycare?" The defensiveness coloring her voice sent him backtracking.

"You could probably do it with one hand tied. That's not—it's just—" He stopped, winced, licked his lips and started over. "Congratulations. I'm sure you'll be very happy here."

"Yes, I will be." Penny's effervescent smile flashed, igniting a glint of excitement in her already joyous expression. "I have so many plans."

"Plans you couldn't carry out as a teacher?" he guessed and knew it was true from the way she peeked at him through her lashes while slowly nodding.

"A public school has restrictions on what teachers can do in the classroom and that's understandable. But Wranglers Ranch is a Christian outreach ministry to kids so it's different here." Her whole face came alive as she spoke. "I believe a daycare that has the same faith and purpose as the rest of the ranch will be a marvelous complement."

"But what about your summer, your holidays?" Rick couldn't fathom why she'd suddenly decided to give up her career.

"Too many holidays are boring. I like to keep busy." Penny's face evidenced no worries. In fact, her enthusiasm communicated itself without words. "This job is my dream. It will be a rush to make Sophie's July first deadline, but we'll do it."

"I'm sure you will, but you can't care for the twins with all you have to do here." Rick made the comment while fervently hoping and praying she'd reject it.

He'd been able to accomplish so much work in the past week, far more than at any time since the twins had taken over his life. He'd even had energy to ride bikes with the twins in the evening, to take them for a picnic on the weekend, to laugh and tease over dinner instead of rushing to accomplish everything before bedtime. Katie and Kyle also seemed more relaxed, happier now that the routine of seeing Penny every day was established.

"I guess I better start looking for someone else to be with the twins," he said.

"Why?" Penny demanded, staring at him intensely. "With you working at Wranglers, once the daycare's open, they could attend here. Wouldn't their transition to here and then school be easier on everyone if they continued with me?"

Rick sagged with relief. He'd tied himself up in knots wondering if Penny had only taken on care of the twins out of a sense of duty to Sophie. Judging by the kids' excitement when he'd picked them up each day, he knew they enjoyed being with her. So now seeing Penny's obvious discontent at the prospect of not caring for them confirmed his hunch that she enjoyed their company and wasn't doing this out of a sense of duty.

"Why would you even think that?" she asked, a hurt tone in her voice.

"I'm thinking of you, Penny," Rick said mildly, hating that he might have hurt her. "I don't want the twins to wear you out before Wranglers Ranch Day Care even opens its doors."

"You, Tanner, Sophie. You're all so worried about me. You must think I'm a doddering old maid. I won't be twenty-eight until August, you know," she protested as red spots appeared on her cheeks.

"Trust me, Penny. When I think of you, I *do not* think of a doddering old maid."

Wasn't that the truth? And the fact that Rick did think of her, a lot, was something he was going to have to correct. His focus needed to remain on the twins and on making the three of them into a family. He couldn't afford to get sidetracked by the pretty woman standing in front of him, no matter how special she was.

"Good to know." Penny grinned cheekily then arched an eyebrow. "So?"

"It's a deal. Katie and Kyle will stay with you," Rick said in a firm tone. "After all, I don't want to—" He paused. Winced.

"Don't want to—?" she prodded.

"I was going to say look a gift horse in the mouth." He peered at her worriedly. "You don't think I'm calling you a horse, do you?"

Penny's hoot of laughter brought the twins running to see what was so funny.

"You came too early, Uncle Rick." Kyle's face wore a fierce frown.

"You don't want to go home with me?" Rick tried to hide his hurt. Obviously he wasn't doing his best at parenting if the kids preferred Penny to him and returning to his un-homey ranch.

"We can't go home till after the bar-cue," Katie explained. "Aunt Sophie 'vited us, 'member?"

"Um—" Confused, Rick looked to Penny to explain.

"That's *barbecue*, Katie." She lifted her gaze to him. "Sophie invited all Wranglers staff including the kids of our soon-to-be daycare clients to a barbecue this evening. I think she texted you about it." Penny ruffled Kyle's hair, smiled when Katie reached to grasp her hand then glanced at Rick. "You'll come, won't you?"

"I guess, though I'm not exactly dressed for partying." Rick glanced down at his dusty jeans. "But I am in the mood to celebrate. I finished a job today. The house will be cleaned tonight and the family can move in tomorrow." Satisfaction created a bubble of energy inside him. "Now I'll have two permanent crews building the cabins here. I'm pretty hopeful that we will finish on time."

Then the bubble burst. Finishing the cabins by his deadline meant leaving Wranglers Ranch, and that meant he'd have to find another caregiver for the twins.

"It must feel wonderful to create a home and so gratifying to know a family will benefit from your work." Penny's generous smile held no undertone but in his mind Rick heard a tiny voice ask, *Like Gillian benefitted from the house you built for her?*

"Yes, it does feel good," he agreed and pushed away the heaviness of guilt.

"So, we're about ready to head over to the patio now. Coming?" Penny waited for his nod, her eyes as bright as the blue cotton sundress she wore. Its full skirt was splashed with the vivid colors of hibiscus flowers. The wind tugged at those flowers, making the skirt swirl around her legs as she walked beside him. The twins raced ahead then ran back to urge Penny and Rick to hurry.

"We're coming," Penny assured them. When they were gone again she addressed him in a lowered tone. "Earlier we were talking about barbecues and I noticed they seem to have memories of outdoor cooking, but they talk as if that was over an open fire. They said it wasn't a wiener roast." Her manner was inquisitive.

"Gillian and her husband were missionaries in a very remote village in Africa," he explained. "The twins were born there and played with the other children. I don't think they ever thought they were any different than the other kids. When Gill first moved back after her husband was killed, she used to joke about having to get used to cooking on a stove again. So my guess is that she prepared a lot of their meals over what we'd call campfires."

"Missionaries. What a life they must have lived." Penny remained silent for the rest of the way, obviously deep in thought.

Seeing that the patio teemed with people and children, Rick snagged a table with benches near the periphery and settled the twins while Penny fetched drinks for all of them. The laughing and chattering quickly died away when Tanner tapped his spoon against a glass.

"Thanks for joining us." He looped an arm around Sophie's waist and drew her near him. "We're getting so busy at Wranglers that we don't often get a chance to just be together. Tonight is that time. We hope you'll enjoy Sophie's good cooking and use this gathering to get to know each other better. And yes," he promised with a smile and a nod at his stepdaughter Beth. "Later we will have s'mores around the campfire. Along with some singing."

"But tonight's main goal is for you to relax and have fun," Sophie added.

"It's our small way of thanking you for being the best staff ever and for making Wranglers Ranch into the outreach facility that our founder, Burt Green, dreamed of. Our success is due to God using you. So thank you for joining us in this ministry." Tanner lifted his glass of punch, and everyone joined in the toast to future success.

Moments later the chattering was once more going full force and the twins along with the rest of the kids were invited to roast hot dogs over the fire. Rick nodded permission and Katie and Kyle scooted off to join the daycare's future clients. He chuckled as they dashed away without a backward look.

"Sophie's gone above and beyond with that feast." Penny inclined her head toward the loaded buffet table. "I don't know how she does it with three kids in the house."

"She's like you. Extremely organized," Tanner said from behind them. "Glad you could make it, Rick. Penny wasn't sure you'd be here."

Rick glanced at her, silently asking why.

"Because you're so busy." She giggled. "And you wouldn't have come if we hadn't brought you along tonight. He didn't read the text Sophie sent," she explained to Tanner.

"I read it," Rick corrected then added sheepishly, "I just forgot."

"Given you're a new dad, I totally understand that issue," Tanner assured him. "Kids provide a steep learning curve for a single guy. Just ask Sophie about me."

Penny's amused laughter did funny things to Rick's midsection.

"I'm glad I came, though," Rick said. It was the truth and his pleasure didn't only come from being with Penny. "After this party I'll have a pretty good idea of who belongs at Wranglers and who doesn't. We don't want trespassers on the job site. My company's priority is always safety."

"Good to know," Tanner approved. "Safety is our priority at Wranglers Ranch, too, because we always have kids coming and going. Seeing what you've both done so far, I'm confident you'll do a great job with the cabins, Rick, and you with the daycare, Penny. But for tonight, please relax and enjoy yourselves." He lifted his hand in a salute before moving on to the next table.

The twins returned with their hot dogs and Penny settled them at the table, insisting Rick retrieve his own dinner. When he returned, he found her talking to a couple whom she introduced as the camp nurse, Ellie, and her husband, veterinarian Wyatt Wright. Then he met Maddie and Jesse Parker. Jesse was one of the youth workers who took a personal interest in ensuring troubled kids had someone to talk to. Both the Wrights and the Parkers had children who would be attending the daycare Penny was organizing.

There were more people, of course. Names blurred

as people kept stopping by to welcome them. Rick was better with faces and figured he'd soon be able to identify every ranch employee. He particularly liked the way people who stopped by greeted the twins and was very proud of the polite way the two responded.

The relaxed family-type atmosphere along with the sheer number of staff and volunteers surprised Rick, but what impressed him most was that everyone seemed comfortable rubbing shoulders with their coworkers. No wonder Penny wanted to work here. An amiable workplace made a world of difference to how you felt about your work.

"Isn't it great?" she murmured when the other adults had moved on.

"What?" He took a bite of his hamburger and savored the succulent beef. "This? It's delicious."

"Actually, I was talking about this place." She waved a hand. "Wranglers Ranch. It's like a little town. Everyone knows each other. Everyone has the same goal—to reach kids. The only difference is our parts in that goal."

A surge of satisfaction filled Rick at knowing he'd be part of it, too. For a little while, at least.

He didn't want to think about after, when he was finished with the work here. He especially didn't want to think about not seeing Penny every day, not being able to bounce ideas about the twins off her or listen to that joyful burst of laughter whenever she found something new to appreciate about life.

Rick had until September 1 when the last cabin needed to be complete. Maybe if he prayed hard enough God would work out a solution for him with the twins by then. Maybe He'd also find a way to erase his guilt over Gillian's death and let him find the same joy Penny had.

* * *

Later that evening Penny sat on a log bench with her shoulder rubbing Rick's as she soaked in the wonderful ambience of worship around the campfire. When Kyle couldn't settle she gathered him onto her knee and hummed along with Tanner's guitar-playing. Rick cuddled Katie the same way and by the end of the song the two were fast asleep.

"Wranglers Ranch has been a life-changing experience for Sophie and me, and for our family." Tanner's voice was quietly reflective as he strummed a background accompaniment.

"We've seen God touch lives in marvelous ways, ways we never dreamed possible," Sophie agreed. "Very soon we'll launch our daycare, which we see as another opportunity to minister to more kids, younger ones this time."

"We'll start with your children, if you bring them. My hope and prayer is that God will use your kids to reach other kids, other parents and other people for Christ." Tanner glanced around the group. "Reaching kids is our mission here at Wranglers Ranch, and Sophie and I are so glad and so thankful that you're on board with us."

"Each of you is blessed with a special gift, a niche of service that God gave especially to you." Sophie smiled at her husband. "I'm sure you've seen the sign over the barn that says, 'Fan into flame the gift that is within you.' Our ranch started with Burt Green and his faith in God's plans for Wranglers Ranch. Burt strongly believed that Tanner could be the means to making his dream happen, but Tanner didn't even believe he had a gift." She smiled at her husband. "I doubt either of them in their wildest dreams could imagine what God has created here today. Perhaps you, too, are astonished at how He is using each of us as an integral part of His work at Wranglers. Don't be. If we're available and willing, God will use us."

Penny met Rick's gaze, unashamed of the tears in her eyes.

"Tears of joy," she whispered when he frowned.

She was startled when he reached out and brushed one off her silky cheek. "You're such a softy," he murmured.

But she knew he was just as moved as she was by the sweet communion of these moments around the fire.

"As we go through summer Sophie and I would like to challenge each of you to fan your own gift into flame. If you see an area where we're missing something, a niche you could fill, a child whose heart burdens yours, tell us." Tanner smiled. "Let's work together to make this the best summer our Wranglers Ranch kids have ever had. Let's make an impact for God. Let's pray for that."

He led them in a prayer of dedication that had Penny's heart singing with excitement at the prospect of joining this ministry.

The Lord will work out His plan for your life.

She'd adopted that verse from Psalms at the beginning of this year, hoping to finally erase the memory of her broken dreams. Yet the brutality of her former fiancé's hurtful denunciation when she'd most needed him still haunted her. Damaged goods, he'd called her before making it clear that he wanted a wife who had more to give him than Penny ever could. His betrayal still hurt.

Thanks to her friendship with Sophie, Penny had

found solace and help when she joined a study of Biblical women, ladies who were also less than perfect and yet they were women whom God used. If God could use someone as imperfect as Mary Magdalene Penny figured He could use her, too. Maybe when she was fully engaged in doing His will the ache inside for a family would fade away.

"Are you asleep like the twins?" Rick's breath brushed against her ear, giving life to butterflies in her stomach. Why did this man have such a strong effect on her senses?

"I'm wide awake." She smiled at him, only then noticing that people had begun to leave.

"Did I disturb your praying?" he asked. "I'm sorry."

"I wasn't praying, Rick. I was just reminding myself that I'm now a part of this wonderful ministry and feeling excited about that." She exhaled, trying to contain her anticipation.

"Good for you but that daycare's going to be a lot of work." A smile feathered across his damaged face as he studied the twins, fast asleep in their arms. "Fifteen or twenty of these guys running around is going to be a challenge."

"Which I'll love," she promised. *It's not the family I wished for but at least my arms won't be empty.*

"Just don't wear yourself out." Rick rose but his gaze remained focused on her. "Listen, Penny, I wanted to ask you—"

Katie wakened and a moment later Kyle followed. Penny suppressed her frustration as whatever Rick had been going to ask was lost in the business of finding the twins' backpacks and getting them belted into his truck. When they were settled, she blew them each a kiss.

"See you on Monday, guys."

They nodded, heads bowing with tiredness.

"Actually, that's exactly what I wanted to ask you." Rick stood behind her, closer than Penny realized as she turned to face him. She stepped back an inch as he said, "Sunday is my dad's birthday. I wondered if you'd like to spend the day at the lake with us. You could swim or boat or just relax if that's what you prefer."

"Water-ski?" The question popped out of her lips without thinking.

"My parents do have a ski boat." He lifted an eyebrow, a tiny smirk flickering at the corner of his mouth. "Does that sweeten the deal?"

"Yes." She blushed at his burst of laughter. "I would very much enjoy going to the lake with you and the twins, Rick. And I love to water-ski so if there's a chance to do both, I will gladly accept. Thank you."

"Good." He thought for a moment. "I'll pick you up at nine?"

"I'll be ready. What can I bring?" she asked, her mind already considering what would be an appropriate birthday gift.

"Nothing. Mom's been cooking for days. She creates this massive birthday dinner for Dad. The chocolate cake is always enough for twenty people so after everyone's had all they want she freezes the rest." He grinned. "She thinks she'll have it for dessert for ages but Dad often sneaks some to have with his coffee without telling her. It's usually gone long before she realizes it."

"Your parents sound like fun," Penny murmured, envious of people she'd never even met. "I look forward to getting to know them. And, Rick?"

"Yes?" He studied her with that serious look she interpreted to mean he expected trouble.

"Thank you for inviting me," she said, and meant it.

"You're welcome. Good night." He waved then drove off.

Penny stood in the shadows and wistfully watched the little family leave. Rick didn't know how blessed he was. He had a forever home to return to, a family where he belonged, roots and strong connections with people who would always welcome him back with open arms and gladness in their hearts.

Penny had never enjoyed any of that. She could never look up her past, trace her family tree or visit a cemetery to find the headstones of relations now departed. Tracing her birth mother had long since proved futile. She didn't belong to anyone.

A familiar pain stabbed deep into her soul. Alone. What a horrible word. Knowing she would never have a family like Rick's, that it could never happen, really hurt.

But God hasn't forsaken you. You're part of Wranglers Ranch now.

Yes, she was. Penny intended to make the staff at Wranglers like her extended family; the ranch would be the home she'd never had. The children of Wranglers Ranch would fill her life and she would pour her heart full of love over every single one of them. No, her life wouldn't be like Rick's, but she was determined she'd make it happy as she managed Wranglers Ranch Day Care.

Yet as she drove home an unspoken question lingered in the recesses of her mind.

Would working at the daycare be enough of a substitute for a family of her own?

Chapter Five

With a substitute teaching her Sunday school class, Penny was able to attend the early-morning worship service before preparing for her day with the Granger family.

Her heart felt light as she sat on her porch, anticipating the low growl of Rick's truck that would signal his arrival. The pastor's message on learning contentedness had Penny counting her many blessings, and a trip to the lake on such a hot day ranked very high on that list.

So did the prospect of seeing Rick again and not as his childcare giver, but as a friend.

Penny realized that she truly liked this man, not only because he poured himself into loving the twins and making their world such a happy place, but also because of his thoughtfulness for his business partner with whom she knew he chatted almost daily so he could keep abreast of their company's situation.

She liked the way he treated his staff, too. Last week she'd watched him from the corner of the day-care playground, had witnessed the directions and then the corrections he provided when a mistake was made measuring out the cabins' locations. Firm, understanding, encouraging. All of those words described Rick.

But most of all Penny liked the way the contractor laughed. In her opinion he didn't do it often enough, but when he did his entire face got into the smile, even the scarred, stiff part of it. And she liked his voice; that low rumble always sent little prickles of awareness up and down her spine. Why did that still happen? Shouldn't she be used to him by now?

"Do you need me to carry this?"

Penny gave a yelp of surprise to realize Rick was right there, standing on her sidewalk, and she hadn't even heard his truck drive up.

"What's in it anyway?" he asked as he hefted the cooler as if it was a free weight. "I told you Mom will have tons of food prepared."

"I know you said that." She didn't explain, simply locked her door and followed him to the truck where the excited twins waited. "Hello, you two. How are you this morning?"

"Good. We're going to Grampa's birthday," Katie explained.

"I know. Isn't it a beautiful day for a birthday?" Penny felt Rick's hand beneath her elbow as she stepped up into the truck. "Thank you."

"Welcome. Did you bring a hat?" he asked with a frown at her blond head.

"And a swimsuit?" Kyle asked. "We always swim when we go to Gramma and Grampa's lake, you know."

"All in here." Penny patted her capacious beach bag then watched Rick climb into the cab and heave a hearty sigh before he shifted into gear. "How long did it take you to pack up?" she asked, hiding her amusement.

"A very long time." His droll voice lent the comment emphasis. "I'll have you know that in the back of this vehicle we have every item anyone could possibly ever need at the beach, in duplicate. Maybe even triplicate."

Penny chuckled then listened as the twins began telling her about the lake. A shared glance with Rick sent her heart rate thumping with a force that dredged up reminders of what happened when she let herself care too much. Getting too friendly was the path to disaster. She would not go there again. Didn't she know by now that there would be no happily-ever-after for her?

Thus chastised, Penny rode to the lake beside Rick but concentrated on the twins, playing I Spy and carrying on conversations that stayed away from personal topics. This wasn't a date. It was an outing to his parents' place. He probably considered it as payment for the time she'd spent watching Katie and Kyle.

He's just being nice. Don't forget that, she reminded herself as they curved around switchbacks and finally arrived at a small lake in the valley of the desert. She exited the truck then took a moment to savor the beauty.

"Welcome, Penny." Rick's father looked like an older version of his son—tall and lean, with the same rugged good looks. His handshake was firm, his dark eyes surrounded by laugh lines. "We're glad you could come."

"Happy birthday," she said, liking him immediately. "I hope you have a wonderful day."

"With my munchkins to share it, it will be perfect." David Granger playfully punched Rick on the arm. "I'm including you in that term," he said before he swung Katie into his arms. He whirled around with her then placed a kiss on her head. "Hello, sweetie."

While he did the same with Kyle, Rick introduced

his mother. Eva Granger was the most extraordinarily beautiful woman Penny had ever seen. She had tawny hair that sprang back from her widow's peak and tumbled to her shoulders in waves and curls. Almond-shaped golden-brown eyes seemed to stare directly into Penny's heart. The elegant planes of her face showed a woman who loved life and embraced every moment. Tall and lean, she wore a belted sundress in off-white that revealed the toned figure of a woman who'd taken care of herself.

"I'm pleased to meet you, Eva. Thank you for the invitation." Knowing she was staring, Penny forced her gaze to span the lake. "This is exactly the place to be when it's so hot. Oh." She tried to hide her surprise when Eva pulled her close for a hug.

"I can't thank you enough for watching the children for my son," she whispered against Penny's ear. "He hasn't looked so carefree since he took over raising the twins." She drew away then glanced at Rick with a loving smile. "You're God's very special gift to the Granger family, Penny."

"Katie and Kyle are delightful." Penny watched with just a little envy as the doting grandmother knelt to fold her loved ones close, her smile so tender.

"Hello, my darlings."

"Too tight, Gramma." After a moment the twins wiggled. Eva laughed and set them free. Her elegantly arched brows rose as she caught Penny watching her.

"Is something wrong? Am I a mess?" She lifted a hand to touch her hair.

"On the contrary, you look lovely. It's just that I have this feeling that I know you and of course I don't because we've never met." Catching Rick's peculiar glance at his dad, she faked a laugh. "Please excuse my fanciful talk. I guess it's being in this gorgeous place."

"I'm glad you like it." Eva glanced around the group. "Swimming first or lunch?"

"Lunch." The decision from the children and the two men was unanimous.

"How did I know they'd say that?" Eva smiled as she invited, "Would you like to help me set things out, Penny?"

"I was just going to ask if I could do something to assist." She walked beside Rick's mother to the sprawling building that faced the lake. "A store, a hotel and your home?" she guessed.

"One building makes it handy for the business, sometimes a little too handy." Eva beckoned. "Come in."

In was a huge open-concept living area added to but separate from the west end of the store. There was a big kitchen, a large table with six chairs and a generous living room whose massive doors led to a patio that overlooked the lake.

"You must love living here," Penny murmured, gazing toward the water. "An oasis in the desert."

"I came from New York so the isolation took a bit of getting used to. But David talked me into giving it a try and I've never regretted it." Her face clouded for a moment and Penny guessed she was thinking about her daughter.

"I'm sure your children loved growing up here," she said quietly.

"Yes, though Rick more than Gillian, I think." Eva paused, swallowed hard then forced a smile. "My daughter talked of becoming a missionary from the day she heard one speak at her church girls' club. She was ten. In the years that followed she never wavered from that goal." Eva wiped a tear from her cheek.

"I'm sorry. I didn't mean to make you sad."

"You haven't, my dear. I love remembering Gilly's dedication to God. I just miss her sometimes." She smiled away her sadness then waved a hand. "This morning I baked some rolls for ham and cheese sandwiches. The twins like those."

"They seem to like most things," Penny agreed. "I hope it's okay that I brought potato salad and some dill pickles. I thought they'd go with whatever you'd planned. They're in a cooler in Rick's truck."

"My dear, you didn't have to buy anything," Eva protested.

"Oh, I didn't. I made the salad last night and the pickles are last year's." She shrugged. "I have a bit of a dill pickle fetish so I make my own."

"How talented." Eva's tiger-brown eyes twinkled. She looked so familiar.

And then the truth dawned.

"Eva McCallum," Penny murmured.

"Granger now. But yes, you're right." Eva calmly continued removing dishes from the fridge. "But that was a long time ago."

"Not that long. No other fashion model has ever had as many covers as you." Penny carried the dishes to the table. "Do you miss modeling?"

"What's to miss? Standing on six-inch heels for hours? Freezing my face into a smile in icy winds off the Hudson River? Holding my pose for eons under burning hot lights in a Soho studio?" The former model made a funny face.

Penny couldn't stop gazing at her lovely face and

thinking how little time had changed it from when she'd seen the magazine covers that one of her foster moms had kept as incentives for her own beauty regimen.

"It sounds like very hard work," she said.

"Yes, it was." Eva laughed then nodded. "And sometimes I do miss that life. But mostly what I miss are the beauty of the changing seasons, the wonderful restaurants and the amazing clothes. None of which I have or need here," she joked. "A swimsuit, shorts and a T-shirt are pretty much my staples now."

"You look beautiful," Penny murmured.

"This?" Eva pinched her cotton dress between two fingers and shrugged. "I made it." She chuckled at Penny's astonished face. "I learned to sew my own fashions when I first arrived in New York. I used to make Gillian's clothes, too, until she went into a jeans phase." A shadow chased across her face before she spoke again. "I still make Katie the odd dress but she's growing so fast. It's hard to keep up."

"And besides all that, this woman is a brilliant cook, a great businesswoman and the love of my life." David wrapped his arm around Eva's waist and kissed her cheek. "I'm very blessed that she gave up her fame and fortune for me."

They shared a look that stabbed a pain straight to Penny's heart. Maybe happily-ever-after was only for other people, people like Eva and David. Sophie and Tanner.

"I brought in your cooler, Penny." Rick set it on the floor. "The kids are washing up. I'm hungry."

"I wonder how many times I've heard that in my lifetime." Eva ruffled his hair. "Fortunately for you I knew you would be and prepared in advance. Let's sit down. Everything's ready except for the kids, Penny's salad and pickles."

"Penny's dill pickles?" Katie licked her lips when Penny nodded. "They're the best, Gramma."

"The best," Kyle agreed.

Blushing with pride Penny set her salad and the container of sliced pickles on the table, somewhat dismayed to realize that the only empty chair was the one next to Rick. She was already too aware of him but she wasn't about to make a fuss. So she took her seat and his outstretched hand, trying to ignore her thudding pulse as David said grace. She had to get these silly reactions under control. Maybe that's what made her yank her hand from his as soon as she heard *Amen*.

The meal was everything Penny had ever dreamed a family meal would be. Filled with laughter, teasing, good food and most of all, love, clearly evidenced as the family caught up on their news.

"Do you have family, Penny?" Eva asked, obviously waiting to serve the cake until the twins had finished their sandwiches.

"I'm an orphan. I tried to trace my mother but there were very few clues and I never had any success." Aware that she'd become the center of attention Penny silently sipped her iced tea while wondering how to change the subject.

"Does orphan mean you don't gots no fam'ly, Penny?" Katie frowned as she asked.

"Yes, that is exactly what it means, sweetheart."

"I'm sorry. That must be hard for you, Penny." David's gentle voice helped ease her discomfort.

"You get used to it," she lied.

"We c'n be your fam'ly." Kyle glanced first at Rick then at his grandparents, his eyes wide. "Can't we?"

"We certainly can. Please do consider us your family, Penny." Eva reached out to wrap her fingers around Penny's.

"We'd love to see you whenever you can come out here," David agreed with a beaming grin that warmed her heart.

"Thank you very much." What a generous family they were. As was Rick.

Speaking of Rick, Penny suddenly realized he hadn't added his invitation to his parents'. She glanced his way and saw he was laughing at something Kyle had whispered and had missed the exchange.

"Now we're all fam'ly at this table." Katie looked delighted by that. "Right?"

"Right." Eva's glowing face seemed to say the more, the merrier.

"Okay so is this fam'ly havin' birthday cake, Gramma?" Kyle snatched another pickle and grinned at her as he crunched on it.

"Do we usually have cake at birthdays?" Rick's eyes opened wide as he pretended surprise.

"Yep. With lotsa candles." Katie frowned at him. "'Member, we had a blue cake for your birthday 'cause you said you liked blue best. Hey, Penny has blue eyes."

An awkward silence yawned when everyone looked at her, including Rick. Penny shifted uncomfortably under his attention.

"She sure does," Rick murmured. His gaze locked with hers and Penny felt a flood of warmth fill her insides. "Very pretty, too."

"I remember that your mother spent eons getting just

the right shade of blue for that icing on your blue cake." David laughed when Rick made a face. "First time I've ever eaten blue cake," he told Penny and pretended to gag. "The twins were a mess."

"It was scrumpy good." Kyle smacked his lips.

"Yeah, and Gramma put things in it. Money and a ring and some other stuff." Katie's lips pressed together and she tilted her head to one side. "I forget what else."

"I don't. Uncle Rick got a button," Kyle said in a gleeful tone.

"A button?" Penny glanced from Eva to David, looking for an explanation. "I don't get it."

"It's a silly old wives' tale. If you find a button in a birthday cake it's supposed to mean you're going to remain a bachelor. I sure hope that's not true." Eva winked at Rick then explained to Penny. "My mother used to do that to the cake when I was a kid so I continued the tradition."

"Because I'm five not twenty-eight." Rick rolled his eyes. "Thanks, Mommy."

Penny couldn't help laughing with the rest of them. Then, just as if she was part of this family, she joined the others in singing "Happy Birthday" as Eva carried in a huge cake with many candles. And she clapped as hard as Katie when David blew out every one.

"No candles burning means no girlfriends, Dad," Rick teased.

"Don't need 'em. I've got my one and only right here." David slipped a hand around his wife's waist and she bent to receive his kiss.

"Keep it that way, buddy," she ordered in a very tender voice as she brushed a fingertip against his nose.

"Yes, ma'am. That won't be a problem," David assured her.

Seeing the love glowing in the couple's eyes brought a lump to Penny's throat. This was what she longed for, what made life worthwhile, what she couldn't seem to find.

When everyone had eaten a portion, or two in Rick's case, of the delicious cake, Eva carried away what remained and returned with a small box, which she handed to David.

"Happy birthday, honey." She smiled fondly as he tore open the package then jumped to his feet and enveloped her in an exuberant hug. "It's a gift certificate to get a gizmo for his boat," she explained to Penny. "He's been wanting a fish finder for ages."

"It's going to be perfect." David tucked the paper into his pocket. "Look out, fish."

"Good choice, Mom. That will go perfectly with my gift." Rick handed his father a brown paper bag. "As you know, I don't do wrapping paper. Happy birthday, Dad."

Penny couldn't swallow past the lump in her throat as she witnessed the obvious love flowing between the father and son. What a fantastic family.

"It's a fishing vest!" David thoroughly checked out every pocket and secret compartment before hugging his son. "Absolutely perfect. Thank you."

"Is it our turn?" Katie asked Rick. When he nodded she and Kyle raced across the room, opened the door and each lugged in a package wrapped as only a young child could with miles of tape securing the ragged edges of shiny red foil.

"Happy birthday, Grampa," they chanted as they handed him the gifts.

"They're games," Kyle said before David could remove the paper. "To play with us."

"Uncle Rick!" Katie wailed. She frowned at her brother. "You're not s'posed to tell. I tol' you that. 'Member?"

"I forgot." Kyle was obviously unconcerned by her irritation as he began a long, involved explanation to his grandfather on the proper way to play Chutes and Ladders.

Next it was Katie's turn to explain her game. While Eva served coffee, Penny rose and removed a small package from her cooler.

"Many happy returns of the day," she said, holding it toward David.

"You didn't need to do that, Penny," he protested. But he tore off the paper just the same then froze, staring at the photo of Rick and the twins that she'd snapped last weekend when the three of them were swinging in the playground and hadn't noticed her. She'd had it enlarged and framed. "It's wonderful," David whispered, obviously moved because there were tears in his eyes when he looked at her. "I'll treasure this. Thank you very much."

"You're welcome." Penny saw Rick lean forward to look. When he turned his head and she met his eyes, an electric current seemed to snap between them.

"You should have taken it from the other side," he muttered under cover of the others' voices, a red flush flooding his face.

"Why?" She frowned at him in confusion.

"The scar—" He broke off as his father thanked them all again.

"Let's go for a boat ride," David said. "After we clean up the dishes."

Everyone pitched in, and cleanup was quickly complete. But after they'd all changed into swimsuits and were in the big boat, zipping across the lake, Penny asked herself the question lurking at the back of her brain.

Why hadn't she taken the picture with the other side of Rick's face in view?

Answer: because she hadn't noticed his scar.

In that moment, as understanding dawned, she was very glad she was wearing sunglasses. She'd taken that photo as she had because when she looked at Rick she no longer saw his scar, because she didn't think of him as a damaged man. When she saw Rick she saw a strong, caring guy devoted to his niece and nephew, a strong son who loved his parents, a dedicated uncle who was focused on making everyone else happy.

Someone who could *only* be a friend.

Rick hadn't water-skied a lot but he knew perfection when he saw it. And he saw it in Penny's lithe figure as she glided across the glass-smooth water, jumping over the turbulent wake of the motor, twisting and turning across the sparkling surface like an acrobatic water sprite.

"She's good," his father commented when their guest finally signaled the end of her ski. He steered parallel with the shore so she could sink gracefully into the water.

"She's very good," Eva agreed. "I wonder if Penny has skied competitively."

"I wanna ski like Penny," Kyle said as they coasted to a stop to pick up their skier.

Using the utmost restraint Rick suppressed his groan. They'd been down this route many times before and he had absolutely no desire to go there again because it always ended with the twins in bitter tears when they couldn't get upright on their skis.

"Uh, I don't think—" He was cut off by Katie.

"Penny can teach us to ski, can't you, Penny?" she asked as that woman swam up to the boat. Firm conviction underlay the little girl's words.

"I could try." Penny smiled at her then glanced at him. Her brows drew together. "Unless you don't want me to," she faltered.

"We've tried before," Rick explained for her ears only as he bent over to take the single ski she'd used. "Without success."

"We have their skis with us. It's a gorgeous day. Why don't we let them try to get up?" Eva's gentle voice softened as she gazed at her now cheering grandchildren.

Rick hesitated but it was really no contest. He couldn't deny Gillian's kids anything.

"Okay, but you two have to promise something." His solemn tone caught their attention.

"What?" Katie eyed him with suspicion.

"That you won't start crying and make a big fuss if you can't get up on the skis," Rick said. He glanced from her to Kyle, trying to make his warning clear.

"It takes a lot of practice to ski, you know." Penny added her cautioning words. "Not everyone can learn right away. Some people try for years and never manage to do it. The thing is to have fun trying."

"I want to learn." Kyle's jaw jutted out in a way that said he wouldn't be deterred.

"Me, too." Katie wore the same determined face only she added firmly crossed arms. "I know Penny could teach us."

Meaning he couldn't. Rick grimaced until Penny's glance met his in a question. But she said nothing, clearly leaving the decision to him. If anyone could teach the twins to ski it would be patient Penny, and he knew that she would handle whatever happened with her usual flair with kids. For confirmation he looked at his dad, who gave an imperceptible nod.

"Okay, you can try," Rick agreed with an inward sigh. "But when Penny says that's enough, we stop. I don't want to hear a word of arguing from you two. Agreed?"

Both kids eagerly nodded.

"Me, first," Kyle proclaimed and jumped over the edge of the boat before anyone could stop him. Thankfully the water was shallow and Penny was right there.

"I'll stay with them." Rick saw his mother glance at his father with a knowing look right before he swung his legs over the side of the boat and slid into the water, too. So what was that about? he wondered. "In case Penny needs help," he told them and pretended not to see Penny's frown.

"Let's go," Kyle urged.

"First we need to talk about when you fall." Penny's voice was serious.

"I'm not going to fall," Kyle said in a cocky tone.

"Yes, you are," Penny assured him.

"Why? Aren't you a very good teacher?" Kyle demanded.

Rick struggled to keep his face straight.

"Actually, I'm very good at teaching people to ski." That was his always unflappable Penny. Wait a minute—*his* Penny?

"Everyone falls at some time or other, Kyle, and it's important to fall into the water properly so you don't get hurt." Penny frowned. "Are you listening?"

"Yes."

So was Rick. He couldn't help it. Penny's teaching voice commanded attention, made you want to hear what she was going to say next.

"So here's what you do. When you fall, lean back on the skis and kind of slide into the water. Let the life jacket hold you up. And most important, when you're in the water you stay right where you are so the boat can pick you up. You don't try to swim to shore," she emphasized. "Understand?"

"Stay where I am." He nodded.

"Good, because that's very important. Second, don't flail around when you're getting up. It's much easier to ski when you let the boat do all the work. Don't try to pull yourself up. Instead you hang on to the rope and keep your legs bent, crouching in the water. Then slowly rise to standing as the boat pulls you. Okay? Show me how you'll do it."

Rick stood beside her, listening to everything she said, admiring her patience as she went over the details three times to make sure Kyle understood exactly what to do and did it. Each time his attention wandered she drew him back with a gentle hand or a soft word. When she was finished she glanced at him.

"Anything to add, Uncle Rick?"

For a minute he got lost in her wide-open gaze. Until she cleared her throat.

"Nope," he managed to say. "Sounds like you've got it covered."

"Okay, then let's see you try it for real." She helped Kyle put on his skis, got the rope in position then stood behind him, her hands holding his waist. "Crouch and slowly rise," she reminded. "And don't lean forward."

His face taut with tension, the little boy held the tow bar with whitened fingers.

"This is going to be fun, Kyle. Relax and enjoy it." Then Penny gave Rick's father a nod and he throttled the engine. "Lean back, Kyle. Good. Now let the boat pull—oh."

Rick caught his breath as Kyle went face-first into the lake. Without a thought he began swimming toward the boy. To his astonishment Kyle was grinning.

"I got up, Uncle Rick. Only for a minute but I got up. Did you see?"

"I sure did, buddy." Rick high-fived him. "Awesome. Want to try again?"

"Yes." Kyle basked under Rick's praise. "I leaned forward," he admitted after a few moments.

"Yes, you did. But you won't do it this time, right?" Penny grinned at Rick. "Okay, here we go." She handed Kyle the rope. "Remember how to crouch?"

"I'll try." Determination was written all over his nephew's face.

"You can do it, Kyle. You're good at this." Penny's repeated encouragement seemed to straighten Kyle's shoulders. As he waited for the boat to line up he looked more confident. "Remember now. The boat does the work. You're going to rise up like a whale and skim across that water."

At Penny's nod, David accelerated.

"You can do this, Kyle," she said just before she let go.

And sure enough the boy rose out of the water and skimmed across its surface.

"I did it," he screamed and looked back toward them. A moment later he was down.

Rick took off in a fast front crawl, heart pounding until he saw the dark brown head bobbing straight in front of him.

"I did it, Uncle Rick! I really did it." Kyle threw his arms around Rick's neck, which ended up dunking both of them.

When they surfaced Penny was there, eyes dancing with laughter as Rick choked and sputtered out the lake water.

"Good job, Kyle. But why did you turn around?" she asked. "You have to keep your attention on the job."

"Want to take a rest and let Katie go?" Rick suggested, thinking *he* could use a break. By contrast Penny looked perfectly comfortable floating in the water.

"Not yet. I want to try one more time. I want to ski longer this time." Seconds later Kyle had hold of the bar and was crouching in the position Penny had shown him, apparently unaware or uncaring that she wasn't behind to support him.

"Very good, Kyle. This time keep your focus on the water. Don't worry about us. We'll be watching." Penny ruffled his wet hair. "Now, have a great run. That's what we skiers say to each other," she added with a wink.

His pride obvious, Kyle's little chest swelled as he called out, "Ready, Grampa."

Rick caught his breath at Kyle's wobbly rise and glanced at Penny, who had her gaze riveted on the boy. He glanced back and exhaled as Kyle regained his balance and went sailing over the water as if he'd done it for most of his life.

"I can't believe you did that." Rick studied Penny with admiration. "I've been trying to teach them for ages and yet in just one lesson you've got him up and skiing like an old hand." He shaded his eyes, following Kyle's progress with a grin. "Look at him go."

"He's a natural." Penny smiled as the boy crossed the boat's wake with just a little bobbling. "Sometimes it's hard for parents to teach kids. I think their worry transfers or something."

"Who taught you to ski?" Knowing Kyle was safe with his grandparents watching every move, Rick floated on his back as he waited for an answer.

"One of my foster parents. He was a famous skier in his day and he loved sharing his sport." Penny floated beside him but her eyes were fixed on something far beyond the azure sky. "When I lived with Chad and his wife, I began to ski competitively."

"You gave it up?" Every nugget of knowledge he gained about Penny made Rick more curious about her past. "Why?"

"Chad and his wife were killed in a car accident. I was moved to another family. They didn't ski." Penny's face altered. "I'm going to swim to that buoy." She took off as if she was trying to outrace a sad memory.

Rick followed at a more leisurely pace, admiring the efficient way Penny moved through the water. She didn't bother when a wave swamped her, ruining her hairstyle. She didn't fuss about her makeup or any of the other things his former fiancée had complained of whenever he'd persuaded her to go into the water. Instead Penny seemed to be in her natural element, enjoying the freedom of movement and buoyancy the water offered. When she reached her goal she turned and swam back toward him.

"What a perfect day," she said as she lay on top of the water next to him.

"Yes, it is," Rick agreed, content with his world as he hadn't been for ages. "Here comes the boat. I guess it's Katie's turn now." He felt a ping of regret for the end of the few special moments they'd shared together.

But what was he thinking? Penny wasn't a date. She was a friend who helped him with the kids. It was getting harder to remember that.

Chapter Six

"It's taking way longer to teach Katie to ski than it did Kyle," Rick muttered to Penny when the little girl flopped into the water for what seemed the hundredth time.

"We can't give up now," Penny shot back and kept up a steady stream of encouragement until finally a very proud Katie managed to rise on her skis and remain upright for several minutes. That she'd matched Kyle was apparently achievement enough for Katie because she soon asked to get back in the boat.

"Rick, why don't you and Penny ski while these two rest?" Eva suggested as she wrapped her granddaughter in a towel.

For Penny, skiing next to Rick on the calm lake was a real pleasure. When he matched her twist for turn as they crossed each other's path and kept his rope free from hers, she knew for certain that he'd had years of experience at skiing. He was a partner in the best sense of the word and she savored every second of that glorious ride. For a few sparkling moments she forgot about being rejected by her fiancé, about her lack of a family and the child she longed for so desperately. For a tiny space in time she pretended the Grangers were her family.

"That was fantastic," she said to Rick when they finally released the rope and glided side by side into the water. "You didn't mention how skilled you are."

"I haven't skied for a while. It wasn't something my former fiancée enjoyed." He signaled his father that they were finished skiing then asked, "Do you have enough energy left to go tubing with the twins?"

"Of course." She grinned, refusing to ask about the former fiancée. *Best day in ages. Don't spoil it.* "Will you come, too?"

"Try and stop me. I love tubing." Rick's smile gleamed white in his tanned face. He was just so good-looking that she couldn't stop her pulse from racing.

Penny concentrated on riding in the inflated tube the Grangers called Big Mable and quickly lost all sense of time as they skimmed across the glassy surface of the lake. Between them the twins shrieked with laughter as they bounced and jiggled over the waves. Penny joined in, sorry when their lovely time together ended far too soon.

"That was so fun," Katie exclaimed.

"Yes, it was. I loved tubing with you guys." Penny hugged the twins close as David reeled in the rope tied to the tube.

"What about with me?" Rick sat on the tube framed by the setting sun.

Quite a picture. She needed to get a grip and stop staring though he stared right back.

"You kept trying to turn us over." To ease the electric moment Penny made a face at him as the twins climbed the ladder into the boat. Then she followed, too aware that Rick was right behind her.

"That's what riding a tube is all about." He sat on the back deck of the boat and crossed his arms over his tanned chest, grinning with smug satisfaction.

"For some people anyway." Eva rolled her eyes at Penny then hugged a shivering Katie close. "Anyone hungry? We've been out here quite a while."

"Starving." David grinned at her then winked at the others. "What?" he said when Rick shook his head. "Driving a boat is hard work."

"For an almost senior citizen, I guess it is," Rick shot back, lips twitching.

The banter between father and son charmed Penny.

"Ha! This almost-senior can out-arm-wrestle you any day of the week, sonny boy," David shot back. "And if you're not nice to me on my birthday you'll have to swim home." He glanced at his wife. "It is time for more birthday cake, isn't it, honey?"

"Later maybe," Eva said. "First we need a fire to roast our hot dogs."

"One fire coming up." David revved the boat into high and zipped them across the water.

Back at the house Penny changed her clothes then found everyone else seated on the deck around a big fire pit, where a fire crackled and spit tiny sparks. The twins seemed happy with their skiing day as they held special forks for roasting their hot dogs.

Eva handed her one, too. "Supper's pretty informal. I hope you don't mind."

"Mind? I love campfires." And Penny did, though she'd seldom had one. It was more the idea of a campfire with its inherent intimacy and sharing that attracted her. Maybe that was why her first attempt at roasting her hot dog ended in complete disaster.

"You put it on wrong," Kyle pointed out, his voice revealing his disgust with her lack of knowledge.

"Do it like this." Katie demonstrated as she anchored the meat sideways.

"Okay. Thank you." Penny blushed under Rick's eloquent but wordless expression.

"Or I could retrieve the one you lost if you prefer your hot dog very well-done," he offered in a droll voice as a teasing smile twitched the corners of his mouth.

"Thanks anyway." Slightly embarrassed, Penny crouched near the flames but quickly backed away from the heat.

"Grampa says you hafta cook 'em over the coals, slowly." Kyle glanced at David, who nodded. "Take your time." He repeated words he'd obviously heard many times before. "There's no rush when you're cookin' hot dogs."

"You've got it, son." David grinned at him then presented Eva with a perfectly roasted dog. "For you, milady."

Penny noticed Rick watching his parents, saw a tender smile lift his lips. The twins watched, too, both wearing fond grins that showed this was a familiar picture to them. Everyone looked so happy to be together. The Grangers were such a loving family. Exactly the kind Penny had always dreamed she might one day be part of. If only...

"I'm very glad you came to share my birthday, Penny." David's warm voice chased away her gloomy thoughts.

"So am I. Very good idea, son." Eva beamed at Rick

then switched her gaze to Penny, her tone more serious. "It's been a pleasure to get to know the woman our grandkids can't stop talking about. Thank you for taking such good care of them."

"They're a joy." A warm glow filled Penny and it grew even warmer when Rick added his tribute.

"I don't know what we'd have done without you." His dark eyes held Penny's until she finally shifted to break contact.

"You would have managed." Like a magnet, her attention kept being drawn back to him.

"We would have, eventually," he agreed. She caught her breath when his grin flashed. She felt warmth suffuse her. "But this is so much better than just managing, don't you think?"

Yes, she did.

Because tomorrow was a workday, Rick suggested they leave after the wiener roast. When many hugs and kisses had been exchanged between children and grandparents, and Penny had promised to return soon, they left the lovely lake. Five minutes into the drive home the twins fell asleep. To Penny the silence in the cab of the truck felt too intimate without their chatter. Uncomfortable and overly aware of the handsome man seated next to her, she nervously searched for a generic topic of conversation.

"Your parents are fantastic. I was stunned when I realized who your mother is," she offered in a chatty tone meant to end the strain she felt from being near him. "She is a beautiful woman."

"She is," he agreed. "I want a wife exactly like her."

"I hope you find her." Penny made a face, covering the rush of dismay that filled her at the thought of Rick married and not sure why it should bother her so. He was a nice man. Of course he would eventually marry. "I doubt there are many women who look like Eva McCallum."

"Granger," he corrected. "But I didn't mean just in the looks department. It's my mom's heart I was referring to. Her capacity for love. I'd want my wife to be like Mom, perfect in every way. I'd hope that together my wife and I would raise our kids with the same unconditional love my parents showed Gill and me."

"So you're thinking of marriage?" she asked carefully while trying to pretend it was an innocent question and that her stomach didn't suddenly feel like it held a rock.

"No." Rick winced then pointed to his scarred face. "My former fiancée made it very clear that no woman would want to marry this."

"Your former fiancée must have been an idiot," Penny blurted then blushed when he stared at her in surprise. "Sorry. I shouldn't have said that. I only meant that most intelligent women have a number of things on their list of husband qualities besides looks, which is usually not number one."

"Really?" He seemed intrigued by her certainty. "What kind of things would you look for in a husband?"

"Love. Patience. Kindness. Things that have nothing to do with a scar." She frowned at his huff of disbelief. "It's true. All of those things are more important to me than looks. But clearly your scars bother you. Couldn't you have plastic surgery?" The words escaped before she could check them. Penny slapped a hand over her lips. "I'm so sorry, Rick. That's none of my..."

"The doctors said they could make the scars go

away." The words seemed forced from him. In the growing twilight, Penny couldn't read his eyes but she knew from the way his fingers clenched the wheel that this was a painful subject.

"You sound like you don't want that." She blinked in surprise when he shook his head. "Why not?"

"Because it would be like pretending the fire never happened," he growled in a low voice. "That Gillian never died in it."

From the faint light of the dash Penny saw a muscle in his jaw tighten. When he didn't continue she sought for understanding.

"So you think erasing the scar means you'll forget your sister?" That didn't sound right and his next words confirmed it.

"I could never forget Gillian. She was my sister and my best friend. I loved her very much." There was a rawness in his voice, an edge that told her the rush of loss and pain was barely tucked beneath the surface. Suddenly a tiny light of understanding dawned.

"You think you should have died in her place." Penny trembled at the glower he shot her way but she couldn't keep silent. This was too important. "That's wrong, Rick, and your sister wouldn't have wanted you to think that way. You know she wouldn't."

"Maybe not. But the least I can do to honor her death is to carry a few scars." His words barely penetrated the quiet of the cab.

"How does feeling guilty honor her?" Penny didn't know all the details and she wasn't sure where this was going. She only knew that blaming himself was hurting Rick and she didn't want him to hurt. He was too nice, too generous, too loving, to the twins.

"It's my way," he said, his tone testy.

"Sophie told me you went into that burning house and saved the twins. That's what Gillian would have wanted. I know from the way you and your parents talk about her and the way the twins describe their mother that to Gillian her children were her most precious possessions and that she loved them dearly. She would gladly have given her life for them. You caring for Katie and Kyle honors your sister in the most wonderful way possible."

"I was there, in the house. I should have saved her." His abrupt response would have ended the discussion only Penny couldn't leave it there.

"You don't get to decide who lives or dies, Rick." She touched his arm. "It's God's decision."

"But I was right there, not twenty feet away. So close." He gulped then continued in a harsher tone. "If only I'd fought through the smoke and got to her, brought her out…"

The anguish in his voice as the sentence trailed away was hard to hear. Penny tried another tack.

"I know it's very hard to accept. But Gillian is better off where she is now, Rick. She's in a place with no pain, no suffering, no more worries. She wouldn't want you to keep blaming yourself for her death."

"You don't know——" Rick clammed up, stiff and rigid in his seat, staring straight ahead.

That was the thing—Penny *didn't* know the first thing about the suffering he endured. She only knew that he was caught in a snare of guilt much as she'd been when her engagement had ended. She could see the weight that burden had etched in the lines around his eyes, could hear it in the sadness of his voice and felt it in the grief he tried to keep hidden but was clearly revealed whenever he spoke of Gillian.

Penny knew this man was stuck, unable to let go of that awful tragedy and move on. He couldn't forgive himself. She didn't understand why that should be. She only knew something inside her insisted she must help him break free.

"You can't change the past, Rick. No matter how long you wear that scar it's not going to bring her back." An urge she couldn't fight insisted she ignore his rock-like visage and keep trying to reach his heart. "Did you ever think that perhaps the scar reminds your parents or the twins of that terrible event?"

His veneer broke when he gave her a surprised and horrified glare. Penny hated the feeling that she'd hurt him. But Rick was such a wonderful, decent, honorable man that Penny couldn't *not* try to help.

"Do you believe that? Is that what they said?" He sounded shaken.

"No one's said it to me. And I'm probably wrong," she said quickly, wishing she hadn't gone down this path. "I don't even notice it anymore. You saw the picture I gave your dad. I didn't even realize your scar was showing."

He glanced at her in obvious surprise, eyes wide. "Really?"

"Really. I'm only speculating, trying to make you see how your insistence on clinging to guilt affects others besides you and colors everything you do." Penny sent out a prayer for wisdom then continued. "You have the twins' futures to think about, Rick. You have to let go of your guilt so you can concentrate on giving them your very best. In and of itself, the scar isn't important unless you dwelling on it hurts them."

After a moment's silence Rick pressed his lips together then switched on the radio. Soft classical music filled the cab for the rest of the ride to her home. Though Penny remained quiet she kept up a barrage of silent prayer for him and the twins.

When he pulled up in front of her house she hurriedly said, "Don't get out. You'll disturb the kids. I can manage."

"Are you sure?" he asked in a brusque tone without looking at her.

She nodded, undid her seat belt then slung her bag over one shoulder. With her fingers grasping the door handle she paused a moment to smile at him.

"Thank you for a wonderful day, Rick."

"You're welcome. We're glad you came." Dutiful but hardly heartfelt. He was upset with her.

Before Penny could lose her courage she reached out and touched his damaged cheek, keeping her hand against the rumpled skin even though he flinched.

"This isn't really a scar, Rick," she whispered. "It's a badge of love. But you don't need it and you certainly shouldn't feel guilty. Anyone who knows you already knows you're the kind of man who keeps his promises to those he loves. Gillian knew. So do your parents and the twins. So do I." She pulled her hand away, opened the door and slid out. She removed her cooler. "Good night," she murmured before closing the door and hurrying into her house.

Inside her home Penny leaned against the closed door, waiting for her heart to slow down as she listened to his truck drive away.

How bold she'd been, touching Rick like that, saying those things. And yet, she'd felt compelled to make him understand that his guilt was needless. Just from today's meeting with his parents Penny knew that they didn't blame Rick. Gillian's death was a tragic accident but it wasn't anyone's fault. So why did he blame himself? What didn't she know about that fire?

Penny hung up her wet suit and towel, put the salad and pickle dishes away then made a cup of peppermint tea and carried it out to her back patio, where she enjoyed the brilliance of the starry summer night. Soon Rick's words replayed in her head.

I'd want my wife to be like Mom, perfect in every way.

The man had once clearly envisioned a family of his own. In light of his fiancée's rejection maybe he didn't think he could still have that, but Penny had a hunch he still thought about being a husband and father. Through the Bible study that Sophie led, Penny had made friends with several women from church. They weren't perfect women, of course. But maybe if she got them together with Rick…

Matchmaking? I'm matchmaking?

"For an honorable, sensitive man who thinks he has to give up everything," she said out loud. Penny liked Rick a lot. If only she—

"You're nobody's idea of perfect," she reminded herself, ignoring the pang of pain that clenched inside at the reminder. "Rick and the twins need somebody special to love them."

That someone isn't you. You're nothing like Eva.

It hurt a lot to accept that. But Penny valiantly swallowed her pain and decided that tomorrow she'd start arranging some *chance* encounters between Rick and potential wife candidates. Naturally they would have to be very special ladies because Rick and the twins deserved the best.

Funny how the thought of him water-skiing beside someone else kept Penny awake long into the night.

"Hello?" On Wednesday afternoon Rick poked his head into the Wranglers Ranch Day Care building. No one answered his summons, which was odd.

"I asked him to meet us at five thirty so you'd have time to get to know—oh, hello, Rick." Penny's eyes widened as she appeared around the corner of the building. She'd requested the meeting so her surprise puzzled him until he got caught up in hugs from the twins.

"Sorry. I'm a few minutes late." He couldn't stop gawking at her.

Penny in yellow was an amazing sight. He'd secretly dubbed it her signature color, bright, full of life and always happy, exactly like her. That was never truer than in the fitted sundress she wore today. It emphasized every curve and showed off her legs so well he had to force himself to stop gawking at her.

Funny how he'd never really noticed women's clothing until he'd seen Penny in the sundresses she often wore. Demure but very feminine dresses that made her seem very ladylike, just like his mom.

"Miranda, this is Rick. Rick, Miranda Soames." Penny indicated the young woman beside her.

"Hello. A new employee at the daycare?" he asked politely as he pulled his gaze away from Penny.

"Oh, no." Miranda, who looked all of eighteen, giggled then gave a gushing smile that unnerved him.

"Penny and I taught together last year. I'm taking over her kindergarten class in the fall."

"Oh. That's nice." Though Rick nodded, inside he was wondering why Penny had asked him to be here at this particular time today. Surely not just to meet Miranda? He chastised himself for thinking that until he glanced at Penny's wide-eyed eager face. Something in that gaze made him wonder. Could she…no. She wouldn't.

"Miranda's really a marvel with kids," Penny said.

She was trying to sell him on the woman. That settled it. Rick gulped, feeling like a worm wiggling on one of his dad's fishhooks until Katie tugged on his arm, diverting his attention.

"Ready, sweetie?" She nodded so he urged, "You and Kyle get your backpacks. We'll leave Penny and Miranda to visit. We need to decide where to go for dinner. It's our eating out night, remember?"

Katie and Kyle raced inside the building with a whoop. Realizing he was now the sole focus of the two women, Rick shifted uncomfortably.

"So the reason I wanted you to be here at this time was to meet Miranda," Penny said, confirming his every fear.

"Uh, okay." He shuffled, trying to rid himself of the jitters Miranda's predatory stare gave him.

"I have some errands to run tomorrow afternoon and can't be here at the daycare. So if you're willing, Miranda has agreed to watch the twins." Penny's smile blazed as if she'd just scored the biggest coup in history.

The way she said it told him everything he needed to know about this appointment but thankfully Rick had just remembered something.

"Uh, that's not going—"

"It's not a big deal, Rick. I can call you that, can't I?" Miranda simpered. There was no other word to describe her syrupy manner. "Penny and I both love children, and your twins are especially cute. We'll have a lot of fun together," she promised him with a gushing smile.

"Well, that's very kind of you but unnecessary as it happens." Rick's awkwardness grew when her vivacious expression suddenly drooped.

"Unnecessary?" Penny frowned. "Oh. Why?"

"Because I'll be taking tomorrow afternoon off for the twins' dental appointments so naturally they won't be here." Seeing Penny's frown, he hurried to explain. "I was going to tell you this morning but you were on the phone when I dropped off the kids and I didn't want to interrupt. It seemed an important call."

"Uh, yes, it was." Penny's cheeks glowed an interesting shade of pink as her gaze quickly veered away from his. "Well, that's all right, then."

"I'm sorry to ruin things like this but I really want to thank you for offering, Miranda," Rick apologized but his thoughts were on Penny. In all the time he'd known her he'd never seen her so flustered and he couldn't help wondering why his change in plans had thrown her off. And what was with that weird way Miranda was gawking at him? Had to be his scar, he decided.

"Another time, perhaps?" Miranda's cheery smile was fading fast.

"Perhaps." Rick shifted uncomfortably. Time, past time, to get out of here. Thankfully just then the twins came bounding out of the building.

"I lost my pig. Me an' Kyle had to hunt for it," Katie explained breathlessly. "But we found it."

"Good. Into the truck now. I'll help you buckle up." When he turned back Penny was glowering at him as if he'd done something wrong. "Um, thanks again for caring for them. I guess you're all ready for the grand opening in a few days, huh?"

"Yes. Everything's in place." Penny bit her bottom lip then blurted out, "If I'm not here the day after tomorrow, is it a problem? Someone else, perhaps Miranda, will be here to watch the kids for you."

"I could get another sitter," Rick offered, confused by her question. "But I thought Thursday was the day you and Sophie planned to hold staff training."

"Oh, yes, ah, that's right." She nodded vaguely, avoiding his stare. "But those plans are sort of—fluid. Anyway, whatever happens the twins will be cared for. I just wanted you to know."

"Okay. Well, thanks. Thanks a lot." The longer Miranda stared at him, the more awkward Rick felt. He left wondering if he looked as confused as those zombies his former sitter had raved about. "So how was your day, guys?" he asked the twins as he pulled away from Wranglers Ranch.

"Good." Kyle immediately began working on the LEGO blocks he was never without.

"It was a funny day," Katie said in a rather solemn voice. He glanced in the rearview mirror and saw her small face scrunched up. "I'm kinda mixed-up."

"What do you mean, sweetie?" Rick asked curiously while thinking Katie wasn't the only one who was mixed-up today.

"I was wonderin' 'bout something."

"What's that, darlin'?" he asked, trying to get back on an even keel.

"Well—do you need love, Uncle Rick?"

"Huh?" With great difficulty Rick kept his focus on the road though he was going to pull into the first hamburger joint he came to so he could figure out what his niece was talking about. "I—uh, I guess we all need love, sweetie." He gulped. If this was parenting, he was about to flunk out. "Why do you ask?" he said meekly.

"'Cause I heard Penny talking to Miss Miranda an' Penny said you needed love so you'd stop hurting." Katie's voice softened. It sounded as though she was near tears. "I didn't know you were hurting, Uncle Rick, but I love you real lots an' Kyle does, too. If we give you a hug will that make your hurt go 'way?"

"I don't think I have any special hurt today, sweetheart, but if I did, for sure your hug would fix it. I love your hugs. I love you and Kyle more than peanut butter," he said, launching into their favorite game in hopes of easing off the subject of his hurts while reassuring her.

"I love you more than peppermints," Kyle chirped.

"I love you more than Christmas trees 'n' candy canes 'n' presents." Katie would never be bested in this game.

Rick responded with only half his mind playing the game as he drove. His irritation ballooned. Penny had said he needed love? What in the world—suddenly a lightbulb clicked on inside his head.

Could Penny be matchmaking? Had to be. But why?

Rick replayed their last conversation on the way home from the lake. He must have said too much and she'd extrapolated from that, decided that he needed a woman in his life. He fought an angry urge to call her up and tell her to butt out—until the questions built.

Why had she thought that? Did he look needy? Did

the twins? Was it so obvious that he was failing as their father?

Tormented by the possibilities that Penny had identified some lack in the twins that he hadn't, Rick pulled into the first fast-food place.

"C'n I have fish?" Katie asked, brows drawn together.

"Fish? Are you sure?" Rick mentally kicked himself for asking. Fish was good for you, way healthier than hamburgers. "Sure. How come you want fish today?"

"Miranda told Penny that's how she gets such long, shiny hair." Katie swung his hand as they walked inside. "I want hair just like hers."

Rick let that go, unwilling to get into the fact that Katie would never have the rich auburn hair that Miranda had.

"Nope, that's not what Miranda said, Uncle Rick." Kyle tugged on his other hand to get his attention. "Miranda said she eats fish caps." His brow furrowed. "Or sumthin like that. I dunno." He shrugged in disinterest. "I want chicken nuggets. An' fries. With ketchup. An' can I have ice cream for d'zurt?"

"As long as you drink your milk," Rick agreed, pleased when they both agreed.

Ten minutes later they were seated at a table, munching on their food, and Rick's anger had lost its steam. Maybe he'd misunderstood. Or the twins had.

"Miranda wants to have babies."

Rick choked on his coffee. It took forever to clear his windpipe. Teary-eyed but finally able to speak he studied Kyle. "Um, how do you know that?"

"She told Penny. Miranda said she wants lotsa kids.

Didn't she, Katie?" He glanced at his sister for confirmation.

"Uh-huh." Katie drank the last of her milk, leaving a wide white mustache on her top lip, which she smeared with a bunch of napkins. "An' Penny said she wished she could have a bunch of babies, too, but it wasn't gonna happen."

"No, she said it was *never* gonna happen," Kyle corrected with his head tilted to one side as if he was thinking about that.

"Oh, yeah. That's right." His niece shook her head then set her innocent gaze on him as a frown marred her pretty looks. "How come Penny won't have no babies? Is it 'cause she don't gots a daddy for them, Uncle Rick?"

"Uh—I don't know." *Be a parent, man. Give a firm answer.* "I guess so."

"Well, maybe if we got her a daddy, she could get lots of babies. Penny'd like that 'cause she loves babies," Katie said around a mouthful of food.

"Uh-uh. Penny said she'd never have babies an' I know why." Kyle looked like a wise old man as he leaned back in his seat confidently.

"Why?" Rick had no business asking that question but he simply couldn't suppress his curiosity about the lovely caregiver of the twins.

"'Cause sometimes when Penny holds baby Carter, she gets tears." Kyle's serious brown eyes met his. "She pretends she's not sad when she gives him back to Auntie Sophie, but she is. That's why she's never havin' babies, 'cause they make her sad."

"Yep." Katie nodded somberly. "They really do."

"Well, you may be right," Rick admitted, surprised

and touched by their perceptivity and concerned about what they'd told him. "I don't know what we can do to help Penny—"

"I do. We can pray." And right there in the local fast-food joint Katie bowed her head and began praying out loud for their caregiver.

A little embarrassed by the public display but also very proud of his niece for her thoughtfulness, Rick added a firm *amen* when she finished her prayer. He bought their ice cream, waited till they'd eaten it then drove back to the ranch, lost in thought. But no matter how he tried he couldn't make his brain stop puzzling over what he'd learned about Penny.

Once the kids were tucked in, Rick threw yet another load of laundry into the dryer. That was when the idea came to him.

Maybe it was Penny who needed a matchmaker.

Pleased with himself, he sat down to make a list of male friends and acquaintances who might fit her bill. Only thing was, he ended up deleting most of them because imagining Penny with any of his rough and tumble buddies gave Rick an unsettled feeling in his stomach.

Must have been the fast food. Certainly couldn't be because he was interested in Penny's personal life.

Chapter Seven

"This grand opening is a zoo," Penny whispered several days later, awed by the number of children and parents milling around.

"You know you love it." Sophie surveyed the room critically. "Are you sure you hired enough helpers?"

"We'll know that by tomorrow, I guess. We have more babies than I expected," she admitted. "After a couple of days I'll have a better idea if Molly is as good as she claims her seven siblings made her."

"She's the newest hire?" Sophie put her hand on Penny's arm to stop her from going to get the girl. "No, don't interrupt her. You can introduce me later. Tanner showed me her résumé, if you can call it that. It's pretty sparse. I was surprised to see that her home address is a shelter."

"Me, too. Do you think I shouldn't have hired her?" Penny had wavered over her ever since she'd offered Molly employment and now new doubts ballooned. "Molly said she really needs a job and she's so willing. She offered to do cleanup or whatever we needed. I thought her soft-spokenness would be an asset, especially with the babies. But maybe I was wrong." Why hadn't she insisted Sophie or Tanner choose the staff?

"She's certainly hit it off with that toddler." Sophie studied the seventeen-year-old as if she was searching for something. "She's so pretty but those baggy old clothes don't do much for her. Not that her clothes matter. I'm sure Molly will be great. It's not that. It's just— I have this weird sense that she's hiding something."

"Like what?" Now Penny was really nervous.

"I don't know." Sophie paused. "Tanner said she's been a regular here for the past couple of months but that she's wary around the horses, worried about falling off, I think he said." She gave a half laugh and shook her head as if to clear it. "None of which has anything to do with her ability to work in our daycare. I'm having opening-day jitters. Ignore me, Penny."

"I'll keep my eye on her," she promised. "But you have to admit, she is a deft touch with the babies."

"That's why you like Molly. Because her mother's heart is just like yours." Sophie grinned then nudged her. "You have to mingle now," she ordered. "The staff using these facilities probably have a hundred questions. I'll get Tanner to slide open the door to the lunch area so folks can pick up a lemonade and a cookie and then we'll have a Q and A session. Is that okay?"

"Perfect." When Penny checked her reflection in the window she saw someone standing behind her and whirled around. "Oh. It's you." She was unnerved by Rick's grin.

"Not much of a greeting for your best customer," he grumbled. "Don't fuss. You look perfect." His solemn brown eyes did a quick scan before he nodded. "Not a hair out of place."

"My hair is always out of place." She mentally ordered her wobbly knees to firm up. She'd known Rick for several weeks. Why was just seeing him still making her weak at the knees? "It's called the tousled look. It's supposed to look like that."

"Yep, you go with that explanation, Penny," he teased then grinned. "Whatever you call it, it looks good on you." He lowered his voice like a coconspirator. "It's not too late to back out, you know."

"Yes, it is."

"Yeah, I guess it is." Rick shrugged. "No reason why you should, either. You'll be great." He stopped, leaned forward to stare into her eyes then asked in an incredulous tone, "Penny! You're not nervous, are you?"

"Well, I am a little—"

"Come on," he chided. "You fearlessly take on two wild twins on a moment's notice, impetuously quit teaching, zip over the waves with only a towline to hang on to and suddenly you're nervous about managing a little old daycare at Wranglers Ranch?" He squeezed her shoulder and said in a very droll Old West tone, "Where's yer backbone, missie?"

"Thanks. I needed that." Penny smothered her giggle just as Sophie called her forward to answer questions.

It took about a half an hour to assure the parents of the children who would use the facilities that a caregiver would be available to watch their children whenever they were needed to work on the ranch and to outline some of the activities they would pursue for different age levels who attended.

"Please feel welcome to stop by anytime to see what your child is doing. We want you as parents to feel comfortable coming and going because that can only help your child settle in and that will ease your minds about them. We want to make Wranglers Ranch Day Care the best place for your child to be, next to home," she added with a grin. "So that's the plan."

She took a few moments to answer questions, though there weren't many. Then Tanner spoke.

"Now we're going to ask you to leave your children with us until noon, so they can get used to the daycare facilities, the workers and their place here. Thank you."

There were a couple of tearful farewells but most of the children were quickly engaged in activities by the staff at different stations around the building. Out of the corner of her eye Penny saw Rick hunker down to speak to Katie and Kyle, hug them then quietly leave. She knew he'd be heading over to work on his cabins.

After ascertaining every child was engaged, Penny entered the nursery room to chat with Molly, hoping to reassure herself that she'd hired the right person. Two of the babies were sleeping. Molly sat in a rocking chair with a third snuggled in her arms. She was softly humming.

"Doesn't seem right to get paid for this," she teased.

"I know." Penny nodded, pleased by the competence she saw. "When you're doing what you love it isn't work at all." She caught her breath as Molly moved to shift the baby, and the rounded mound of her stomach clearly showed. "Molly, are you pregnant?"

"Yes." Apprehension grew in Molly's rounded face. "Does that mean I can't work here?"

"No, of course not." Penny rushed to reassure her. "We hired you because we thought you had a way with kids. And you do. Look at you."

"But you don't like that I'm pregnant and not married." Molly nodded sadly, defeat in her voice. "Because you think God doesn't like it. I get that. Can I just stay for today?"

"Molly, I don't want you to leave." Penny touched her arm to reassure her. "I'll have to tell Sophie and Tanner, of course. But I don't see why you can't continue working here. Unless your doctor says otherwise." She waited for the girl to respond but Molly wouldn't look at her. "Did you ask him?"

"I don't have a doctor." Molly lifted her head, her eyes defiant.

"But surely—" Penny stared at her then gulped as the truth blazoned across her face. Molly was alone, just as she was. "Not even when you first learned you were pregnant?" she asked hopefully then sighed when her newest employee shook her dark head. "Molly, honey, you have to see a doctor to make sure you're doing everything you need to for the baby."

"Doctors cost money. I don't have money for that." The fear in her voice pained Penny. "I can't stay in the shelter for much longer so I need to save my money so I'll be able to rent a place. Anyway, I'm healthy. So is the baby."

"You can't know that," Penny insisted. "Besides—"

"I'll leave." Molly rose and handed her the baby. "Maybe I can get a job somewhere else. I got As in my childcare course in high school. I'm not stupid."

"I know. That's why we hired you." Penny set the sleeping baby in a crib then faced the frightened girl. "Please wait, Molly. Let me talk to Tanner and Sophie and find out what they suggest. Maybe they know of a place you can rent. Wranglers Ranch has a nurse named

Ellie Wright. She might know a doctor who would help you."

"I don't know." Molly frowned. "I don't want charity." Her eyes flashed and her chin jutted out. "I just need a job."

"Which you have," Penny assured her. She placed a hand on her shoulder and squeezed. "You keep doing your job. I'll figure out the rest." She glanced at Molly's stomach. "I only want to help you do the best for your baby and for yourself. Okay?"

Molly slowly nodded.

"Good. Now I'd better check on the others. Can you handle these three until Dora comes back from her break?"

"Sure. I used to babysit triplets. Three babies the same age is lots harder than watching these three." After a moment her face fell and she looked away from Penny. "I didn't do anything wrong," she whispered.

"I know you didn't." Penny waited, sensing Molly needed someone to talk to.

"A friend of my Mom's—I babysat his kids. He attacked me one night. I couldn't fight him off." Tears welled. "My mom didn't believe me. She said I was lying because I didn't like them being together. I refused to babysit for him again and that made her really mad. But I couldn't go back there," she wailed.

"Of course you couldn't," Penny empathized.

"Well, anyway, when I found out I was pregnant, my mom said I had to have an abortion. But I couldn't do it. It's not the baby's fault," Molly said fiercely then quickly hushed after a glance at the sleeping infants.

"Of course you couldn't do that. Not the way you

love babies." Penny drew the weeping girl into her arms and tried to comfort her while anger stirred within her.

"I ran away so she couldn't make me. That's why I didn't finish the childcare course." Molly sniffed. "I've been so scared. I only had a little money saved up and now most of it's gone. That's why I stay at the shelter. But I don't want to be a mom. I don't want a baby." The young girl pulled free in order to dash the tears from her eyes. "I couldn't let it die, I had to run away. But it's so hard to be al-lone," she hiccuped.

"You're not alone anymore, Molly. You have Wranglers Ranch and you have me. Together we'll figure something out. I don't want you to stress about it anymore. Okay?" Penny smiled to reassure her, waited till she was calm then left the room.

Penny's heart boiled with fury. She stepped outside to reclaim her control and to whisper a prayer for help for Molly. How ironic this situation was. Here was a girl who was going to have a child she didn't want. And here was Penny, eager and ready to be a mom but unable to have the child she longed for.

Why, God? her heart whispered for the umpteenth time.

"Penny?" Rick stood beside the fence surrounding the daycare playground. His forehead furrowed as he frowned at her. "Are you okay?"

"No," she admitted. "I'm angry and frustrated and fed up and—"

"Need a coffee break," he finished with a smile. "Wanna join me?" He held out a hand.

There were a hundred jobs she needed to complete, fifty items on her to-do list that screamed for immediate attention, but Rick's invitation was just too sweet to ignore.

"Yes, I do want to join you for a break. Thank you. Just let me make sure the others know where I'll be." She summoned a smile before hurrying inside.

She'd expected to return and find he'd headed for the patio where Sophie always made sure there was coffee, iced tea or lemonade for staff who needed a break. There were usually snacks, too, leftovers from her most recent catering job.

To Penny's surprise, Rick was still waiting for her by the gate, leaning against the fence, his arms crossed over his chest as he peered at the cabin he'd begun constructing.

"Something wrong?" she asked as she joined him and they began walking toward the patio.

"Yeah, there is." He fell silent.

"May I guess?" Penny didn't wait for his answer. "You don't like the way the cabins are going to face." She chuckled at his surprised look. "I checked out some of the houses you've built. You like to create something unusual in each one. The cabins are going to be lovely but each of them will be the same as the next, without that element of surprise you always go for. Am I correct?"

Rick nodded, waited until she'd poured herself an iced tea and selected a muffin. He chose coffee and a treat for himself before joining her under the lacy branches of a mesquite tree that provided shade but also allowed a cooling breeze.

"You've looked at my work?" His surprise was obvious.

"Why wouldn't I? Aren't you proud of it?" she asked with a teasing grin.

"Yes, but—" He chewed his doughnut thoughtfully. "Got any ideas?"

"As it happens, I do." Penny snickered at his rolling eyes. "Well, you did ask."

"True." He sipped his coffee then leaned back. "So tell me your thoughts, Penny."

"Actually, I've been thinking about those cabins of yours quite a lot," she said, hoping he wouldn't take offense at what she was about to suggest. "The design is for all of them to face a central area, correct?"

"Yes." Rick nodded, wondering how and when she'd seen the plans. "A courtyard."

"So here's my idea. What if they didn't? What if each one opened in a different direction?" Penny quickly sketched a rough outline of her thoughts on her napkin. "Then each front door could offer—"

"Its own unique perspective on the desert." He nodded. "Very good. And if we replaced a few of the barrel cactus here and planted a couple of saguaros beside the front of each one, it wouldn't be long before the cabins would look like they'd been there forever. Problem solved," he said with a surprised look. "Thank you."

"You're welcome." A little shiver crept over Penny's skin when Rick grinned at her. Scar or no scar, the man was an absolute hunk. "Now maybe you can help me with my problem."

She didn't understand the odd look that washed across his face or his hesitation, but once he said, "Sure," she told him Molly's story.

"I want her to see a doctor and soon."

"Do you know her due date?" Rick stole the corner of her uneaten muffin. He looked so calm.

"No." Penny leaned back on the bench. "I'm so furious at her attacker I'd like to spit. My mind's fixated on him and what he's done. He should be made to pay for assaulting that girl." She pursed her lips. "Molly should go to the police."

"Maybe." Rick swirled his coffee, his voice thoughtful. "But from what you've said about her reaction, it doesn't sound like she's after retribution. Sounds more like she's focused on finding a place to live." He frowned as he studied her. "I know you're upset for her, but maybe you have to forget about him and concentrate on what Molly needs."

Penny thought for a moment about it then smiled. "Yes, you're right. You're very good at this parenting thing, you know."

"I am?" Rick's startled gaze searched hers. "Why do you say that?"

"Because of your focus, which is on Molly," Penny said with a reassuring smile. "That's what parents do. They focus on the child's needs. Thanks for reminding me." She checked her watch and rose. "Guess my coffee break's over."

"Mine, too." Rick also rose.

They stored their used dishes in a nearby bus pan then ambled back to the daycare.

"I have no idea how to go about finding Molly a home," Penny muttered. "Guess I'll talk to Sophie and some friends to ask their advice."

"Friends like Miranda?" Rick's knowing stare made her blush. "I don't want to date her, Penny. Or anyone else. I've got my hands full with the twins and my construction company. Please don't try to matchmake for me."

"But you—"

"I have a couple of single friends who really need a woman in their lives," he mused in a firm, clear voice with subtle undertones. "Want me to introduce you to them?" Rick tilted his head to one side, watching her blush deepen.

"Okay. Point taken," she whispered.

"I could only ever settle for the perfect woman, Penny," he said very quietly. "Since she only exists in my imagination, I'll remain single. I haven't got time for romance anyway. I can barely keep up with the twins."

"Got it." She paused at the gate to the daycare. "I'm sorry."

"It's okay. You and I are peas in a pod, determined to get through the life God's given us on our own two feet. We're strong, Penny. We can manage the future without help. We don't need a partner." He tossed her a funny, lopsided grin then walked to his work site.

Penny remained in place watching Rick for a few minutes and wishing he hadn't said that. Because she wasn't determined to go through life on her own. She didn't want to manage the future on her own. Okay, maybe two failed romances had made her give up on her own happily-ever-after, but she still longed to share her life with a child. Maybe it was time to dig deeper into adoption.

A child's yell of frustration forced Penny to shelve her daydreams of motherhood and get back to work. But no matter how hard she tried or how busy it got, she couldn't put handsome Rick out of her head.

Easy for him to shrug off the need for a partner. He had the twins.

What did she have?

Chapter Eight

By mid-July Rick finally saw major progress in his work. Two of the contracted cabins were almost complete and a third had its adobe walls in place and was waiting for clay shingles. Foundations for numbers four through six were poured and his confidence about meeting his September first completion date was growing.

It had become commonplace for him and Penny to chat about the cabins when he dropped off or picked up the twins or when they shared a coffee break or lunch together. Her ideas intrigued him. Yesterday she'd asked him about colors. When he'd explained that all the cabins would have the same muted values, Penny had suggested slight variations in color that would make each building easier for young campers to identify. She seemed interested in the construction, too, and had offered several ideas, some of which Rick had used.

The window seat, for instance.

In memory of Gillian and her love of grand vistas Rick had installed a big picture window that overlooked the desert in the second cabin.

"It's a gorgeous window. You're going to put in a window seat, right?" she'd asked him.

"Hadn't thought of it."

"Oh, you have to. A window seat would offer the perfect place for a counselor to sit and talk to campers about God." Penny had been so enthused about that.

Her idea reminded Rick of the one visit he'd made to see his sister and her husband in Africa. He'd watched in amazement as Gillian tenderly ministered to suffering women. This window reminded him of that time so he'd incorporated Penny's window seat into the cabin's design.

But despite her assurances that the cabins were fantastic, Rick worked with a constant tension, determined that nothing would go wrong in these cabins as something had gone wrong in Gillian's home, something that authorities now believed had caused the fire. Something they seemed intent on blaming on him.

He shrugged off the worry and remembered that yesterday Penny had suggested installing a skylight in the fourth cabin.

"Too hot in the summer," he'd argued but she'd already considered that.

"It wouldn't face the sun if you slanted the roof north a bit more," she'd countered. "Don't manufacturers make skylights that open? An opening in the ceiling would let out the heat at night."

Today as they met for their coffee break, she spotted the frame on the roof that said he'd taken her advice. Her face beamed in that irrepressible *Penny* grin.

"It's going to be sweet to stay in that one, Rick. Campers will love it."

"That's the goal." Her words sent a rush of satisfaction through him. He picked up a cup, ready to serve her. "Coffee this morning?"

"Iced tea. I need to cool down. The kids are really antsy today." Penny accepted the brimming glass he handed her, took a sip then added extra ice from a big thermos. After selecting a shiny red apple, she walked to a table in the shade. "How are you and your crews faring in this heat?"

"Okay. We take turns at finishing work on the inside every so often. It's cooler there." He poured two more glasses of iced tea and drank one immediately before following her to the table with his second glass and a selection of fruit. "We've got the patio to ourselves today."

"For once." Penny studied him with that curious expression that always preceded her questions. "I'm usually here by six in the morning but lately I notice that you always seem to have arrived before me."

Rick smiled. Penny always had questions for him. There were a thousand things she wanted to know. That was all part of the wonderful eagerness with which this woman dove into life.

"I've seen the twins dozing in the truck while you wander over the site, Rick. What are you looking for?" She bit into her apple while she waited for his answer, apparently unaware of the tension that suddenly gripped him.

"Oh, I'm just checking that there aren't any mistakes or problems someone's missed." He strove for nonchalance, shrugging as if his intense inspections barely mattered—which was far from the truth. They mattered so much. "I can't leave anything to chance, Penny. These buildings are important to Wranglers

Ranch. Also, it's my company's reputation that's on the line so I want everything perfect."

"Is any building job ever perfect?" She sipped her tea while keeping a steady bead on him.

"This one is going to be as perfect as I can make it," Rick promised her, aware that she'd noticed the sudden tightness of his voice. He savored a spear of chilled pineapple, half wishing he hadn't joined her today. There was nothing better than sharing coffee time with Penny, except when she asked questions he didn't want to answer. The woman was relentless at learning the truth.

"Do you often have problems on a work site?" She frowned at the bruise on her apple.

"There's always something." Rick strove to sound vague.

"But you have inspectors who have to approve each stage, right? They'd catch a big issue." Penny raised an eyebrow as she waited for him to respond.

"I hope so." *Change the subject, man.*

"And yet you keep checking everything yourself, every single day." She kept looking at him until he began to wonder if she could see right inside his brain.

Rick shifted uncomfortably. Much as he enjoyed these times with Penny, he didn't want to talk about Gillian's death yet once more.

"You've got that look again," Penny murmured.

"What look?" He pretended that he was both surprised and indifferent, hoping she wouldn't keep pressing him. As if! This was Penny, after all.

"I'm not sure how to describe it." She rested her elbow on the table and cupped her chin in her palm the same way Katie did when she was mentally puzzling over something. "It's the sort of look that says *I'll do my best at this or die trying.* Sort of like that." She pondered his face with a curiosity that wasn't going away soon. "Are you having problems with this job, Rick?"

"No." Which actually meant *not yet.*

"But you expect some." Penny was so intuitive.

"I anticipate problems with every job," he temporized. Maybe he could still head her off. "Throughout construction I keep checking everything, sometimes twice, to make sure nothing goes wrong. I don't want children hurt in any of my structures. Or anyone." *Anyone else besides Gillian*, his brain added.

"No, of course you don't." She seemed to be mulling that over, which allowed him to change the subject.

"How are things going with Molly now?"

"Good, I guess. It's odd." Penny frowned. "She's going to be a mother in a few months but she seems totally uninterested in her baby. All she talks about is getting a permanent place to stay, finishing her education, stuff like that."

"Maybe motherhood doesn't seem real to her yet or she doesn't want to dwell on how she became pregnant." Rick shrugged when Penny grimaced. "Or maybe being homeless really bothers her. Staying in the shelter can't be easy." He sipped his tea.

"I know it can't. That's why I invited her to stay with me." She chuckled when he jerked around to stare at her in astonishment. "I have three bedrooms, Rick. Truth to tell, I wouldn't mind the company. But Molly refused."

"Why?" He couldn't fathom why anyone who was homeless would refuse to stay with someone as nice as Penny.

"It has to do with her boyfriend, I think. From what

she's said, it sounds to me as if he wants them to find a place to live together. He's telling her they need to be more independent or something like that." Penny's face perfectly expressed her thoughts about that. "As if being seventeen, alone and living in a shelter isn't independent enough."

"What does this boyfriend do?" Rick finished off his last bite of orange.

"His name is Jeff and I haven't yet discovered that. But I doubt he has full-time employment." Penny twisted her head to look at him in that way she had that made him catch his breath and worry. That look that said she was mentally assessing him for something.

"What?" Now why did he ask that? It would only encourage her.

"You don't have an opening on your crew, do you?" Her inspection intensified. "Maybe if Jeff got a job..." Her voice drifted off. Her brows were raised as if in a question, only he didn't understand what that question was.

"You're not matchmaking again, are you, Penny?" Rick backed away when she pretend-punched his upper arm. "Well, you did it before."

"I'm simply trying to come up with a way to help Jeff," she clarified in an injured tone.

"Uh-huh. The same way you tried to help me?" Rick nodded and grinned, knowing he was right. Helping was what Penny did. She helped everyone, all the time, all she could. She was truly amazing.

"Tanner doesn't have any openings at Wranglers. He said to ask you." Her stare caught and held him, demanding a response.

"Okay." Rick heaved a silent huff of unease at the

thought of a neophyte among his practiced crew. "You can tell Molly to send Jeff to see me, but he should know up front that he'll be a gofer and that it's hard work, harder in the heat."

"Thank you." She grinned as she jumped to her feet, arms outstretched. "You're one of the good guys, Rick. Bless your heart."

He thought she was going to hug him, even anticipated it with a great deal of pleasure. But as if suddenly aware, Penny apparently rethought the gesture, grabbed their glasses and rushed toward the bus pan, leaving Rick wishing she'd followed through on that impulse.

Being hugged by Penny was an experience he'd often envied the kids because Penny threw her heart and soul into affection. Which reminded him of Kyle's insistence that she wouldn't have kids because they made her sad. Rick figured he knew Penny pretty well, enough to know that a little sadness wouldn't stop this woman from embracing a child, any child.

Apparently it was only him she couldn't embrace. He didn't like that. Not at all.

Well aware that Penny took her time returning to their table, Rick noticed that when she did, her cheeks were pinker than they had been when she left and she avoided his gaze. He could have spent the afternoon looking at her but his phone chirped, interrupting that pleasure. When he read the message, Rick's world immediately lost its shine.

He felt weighted down by the text message as they walked back to work. By contrast it seemed to Rick that Penny almost floated. She always moved gracefully yet very energetically no matter how hard she'd been working. Did nothing ever get this woman down? he wondered as he wiped his forehead.

"I have some ideas for the next cabin." She gave him a cheeky grin when they reached the gate to the day-care. "Want to hear them over supper tonight? I've got some ribs in my slow cooker at home that I'd be happy to share."

Rick decided to get his favor asked first.

"That sounds good. Thank you. We'd love to. But we'll have to leave early. I have to make uh—er, a run to Phoenix tomorrow." He hurried on, hoping she wouldn't ask why and that made him feel guilty. "I don't expect to be late, but I could be. Is it a problem if the kids stay here a little longer?"

"Of course not. That's the whole point of Wranglers Ranch Day Care—to be here when we're needed. But I thought you worked with a Tucson supplier. Won't they bring in the building supplies you need?" This very smart lady would soon know all his secrets.

"Mostly they do. But this is something else. So it's not a problem?" he repeated.

"Not at all. But if you don't know your schedule, why don't the twins come home with me tomorrow?" she offered with a smile. "That way you can be as late as you like and I'd have some company."

"Like a sleepover?" Rick frowned at that idea. Since Gillian's death he hadn't even left the twins at his parents' overnight because Katie and Kyle often woke with bad dreams and he didn't want to disturb his dad's already short nights in the busy summer.

"Exactly like a sleepover." Excitement filled Penny's face at the prospect. "They can stay overnight and I'll bring them back to Wranglers Ranch in the morning. You'll see them when you come to work."

Penny looked so enthusiastic, Rick hated to refuse. And why should he? She'd know exactly what to do for a nightmare and it would help him mightily. Also, his absence would probably be like a holiday for the twins. In fact, he had a hunch they wouldn't even notice he wasn't there with Penny in charge. God had certainly done him a favor when He'd placed Penny in their path. Now if He'd only do something about the situation with Gillian's fire.

"Rick? Would it be okay?" she asked anxiously.

"It would be wonderful and really nice of you." Why didn't this woman get married and have six kids of her own to love? And why did that thought make his gut clench? "I know Katie and Kyle will be ecstatic."

"I'm just like them," she said, gleefully rubbing her hands together. "This is going to be so much fun." She stopped at the door and waved. "See you later."

Rick lost his smile as he waited for Penny to enter the daycare before moving on. If only his world could be rectified so easily. But judging by the message from his lawyer, it was time to face up to his mistake, the one that had cost Gillian her life.

Too bad Penny couldn't help him with that.

That evening after Rick and the twins had shared her supper and then left, Penny spent hours making plans for the twins' sleepover. Rick had warned her that the two might waken in the night so she made sure there was a night-light in place and that there were plenty of treats in her cookie jar.

But at work the next day she was still trying to ensure everything would be perfect for this, her first attempt at motherhood. Penny desperately needed this sleepover to be successful because she'd decided that if she could handle this she just might be able to handle adopting a child.

"You've been singing all day," Molly noted when all the children had been picked up, except for the twins. "Like a kid who's about to get inside a candy store."

Penny blushed and explained. "I've never done this before. I hope we manage okay."

"You'll be great. Kids are your life," Molly said.

If only that was true.

She took the twins home, fed them and played games until bedtime. When Rick called her cell Penny felt a burst of pleasure.

"Are they sleeping yet?" he asked.

"We just finished reading a story about Jonah and the whale. Would you like to say good-night?" she asked, heart racing at the sound of his voice.

"Please."

She pressed the speaker button then held out the phone so the twins who cuddled ear to ear could listen.

"Hi, guys," he said in a cheery tone. "What's up?"

"We had pie for supper, Uncle Rick." Kyle licked his lips in remembrance. "Strawberry," he added. "With ice cream."

"Did you save any for me?" Rick's voice asked over the speakerphone.

Kyle looked at her in question. "There's some left over," he said in an excited tone when Penny nodded.

She smiled when Rick loudly smacked his lips. The twins giggled wildly at the noise before telling him every detail about their day. When at last Katie and

Kyle finished their good-nights Penny told Rick she'd call him back after she'd tucked them in.

Once that was done, she carried a cup of peppermint tea to her favorite chair in the living room and snuggled into it, a quiver inside betraying her eagerness to hear his voice again.

"Everything okay?" he asked her.

"Fine. I think they're already asleep." She liked that the twins were uppermost in his mind. "Did you have a successful day?"

After a very long silence he said, "I don't know that I'd call it that. It was a long meeting. That's why I'm driving home so late."

"You shouldn't be talking if you're driving," she worried.

"It's hands-free. How was your day?" he asked and suddenly Penny found herself sharing her day just as the twins had, something she'd longed to do ever since her broken engagement.

"It seems so odd to me that Molly's so uninterested in her baby. I've asked her questions, suggested I hold a baby shower, done everything I can do to get her to discuss the future but she doesn't respond." She sighed. "I don't get it. If that was me and I was going to have a baby, I'd be talking about it nonstop."

"Yes, but we all know you're a little over-the-top when it comes to kids," he teased. He was silent a moment then asked, "Do you think she might be trying to stay disinterested on purpose?"

"Why would she do that?" Trust Rick to look at it from a different perspective.

"You said before that Molly doesn't seem interested

in the baby. Maybe that's because she doesn't intend to keep it."

The words pinged against Penny's conscience like rocks hitting a wall.

"Of course," she murmured. "That's it. She's been saying she doesn't want to be a mother. She's going to give up the baby for adoption. She doesn't want to let herself get too close because she's afraid she won't be able to let go when the time comes. You're a very smart man, Rick Granger."

"You can say that as many times as you like," he teased.

"So how do I help her with that?" Penny wondered aloud.

"I love that about you, Penny. You immediately jump into caregiver mode. You've got such a great heart."

He *loved* that about her? What did that mean?

Stunned into silence, she sat there, cradling the phone, trying to make sense out of her whirling thoughts.

"Penny?"

"Yes?" She cleared her throat. "Sorry. I'm here, Rick. Just thinking."

"About?"

Was it just her or did the conversation suddenly seem to feel very intimate?

"My life. Or lack thereof." As she sat in her dimmed living room, the possibilities for the future expanded as Penny began to imagine her dreams coming true. She was jolted from her thoughts by Rick's irritated voice.

"Lack? What does that mean? Come on, woman. I'm driving on this uber-busy highway from Phoenix," Rick complained. "Don't make me pull off so I can concentrate on squeezing an answer out of you."

"I'm thinking that if Molly wants to give her baby up for adoption, then maybe—" Penny hesitated, suddenly uncomfortable and unsure about telling Rick.

"Maybe? Go on," he urged.

Something inside prompted her to continue. Surely Rick would understand?

"Maybe I could adopt that baby." There, she'd said it, and with the words came a huge rush of hope. Surely this was part of God's plan. Maybe that was why He'd sent Molly to Wranglers Ranch.

The lengthening silence on the phone worried her. "Rick?"

"Yeah. I'm here." There was a pregnant pause before he asked, "Is that really what you want to do, Penny?"

"Yes. I want to be a mother more than anything." The words slid out without thought, so deeply ingrained was her desire.

"Then why don't you have your own kids?"

Penny held her breath for a moment, hesitating, unsure of baring her heart to him. But Rick was her friend. You didn't lie or pretend to real friends. Friends laid out the truth because a real friend was on your side. A real friend would support you no matter what.

"Is the connection bad? I can't hear you, Penny," Rick said a little louder. "Did you hear me? I asked why you don't have your own kids."

"Because I can't," Penny told him.

And heard only silence in response.

Chapter Nine

A week later Rick could still hear the echo of that conversation in his head.

"I asked why you don't have your own kids."

"Because I can't."

Can't? As in didn't want to raise them alone or was afraid to be a single mom or couldn't afford it or… A thousand scenarios had played through Rick's brain since that phone call but none of them satisfied his need to understand Penny's motivation to adopt.

He would have pressed for an explanation that night but there hadn't been time because Katie had cried out in her sleep and Penny had ended the call without explaining. Assuming she'd need time to settle Katie he'd waited and then it seemed too late for phone calls.

Rick had hoped Penny would clarify her comment the next time they met for coffee at Wranglers. But that hadn't happened, partly because he'd been so busy and partly because she was, too. So he figured maybe church on Sunday might offer an opportunity to talk, but Penny hadn't brought up the subject there, either, meaning he was no closer to learning what she'd meant.

Given Penny's less than exuberant state the past few days, Rick now wanted to know the answer more than ever. It seemed to him that she'd lost some of the zip he'd so admired during their coffee times. In fact, the past few days he'd assumed she was avoiding him because on the occasions he'd asked at the daycare he'd discovered that she had either finished her break before his or hadn't taken one. When he spotted her on the grounds at Wranglers Ranch she merely waved and kept going and on the only occasion they had chatted she'd offered no suggestions for the newest cabins. When he picked up the twins, it was always Molly who waved them off.

Something was definitely wrong with Penny, and Rick intended to find out what it was. Wasn't that what friends did?

"Hey," Rick greeted her that afternoon, having waited eons beyond his regular break time, leaving his crew to manage on their own specifically so he could speak to her face-to-face. "You're a hard lady to catch."

"Oh, you were looking for me?" She pretended surprise but there was a glint in her eyes that told him she wasn't thrilled about being cornered. "What do you need?"

"Nothing. I wanted to ask if you'd come to dinner on Saturday evening. My parents are going to be in town and I thought we'd barbecue. Dad's good at that." Rick grinned, striving for lightness, something to diminish the shadows that filled her expressive blue eyes. "Nothing fancy but we'd love to have you join us."

"That's very kind of you, Rick. I'd like to come but I'm not sure about Saturday." The old Penny would have jumped at the chance to spend more time with the twins. Either they were wearing thin or something was off. "May I let you know tomorrow?"

"Sure." He pretended to check his watch though he was fully aware that he'd been sitting here far longer than he should have been. "Time sure flies. Guess I better get back to work. Everything okay with the twins?"

"Yes, or else I'd have told you." She frowned, studied him and asked, "Is everything okay with you?"

"Same old same old." He rose.

"Katie says you've been on the phone a lot and Kyle's worried that you're worried." Penny's brow furrowed as she studied him. "Anything I can help with?"

This time Rick was the one feeling cornered.

"Work problems," he said with an airiness he didn't feel. "It will take time to sort out." *Years of time in prison*, he thought and winced.

"You're sure?" Penny noticed. "The twins are really concerned about you, Rick."

"Because I burned the bacon this morning," he joked. "I got caught up in a phone call."

"Kyle said it was an argument. Something about their mother." She didn't break her stare, eyes boring into him, searching.

Rick swallowed, trying not to look guilty. He so didn't want to go into this with her.

"You know you can tell me anything, don't you? I'd never pass it along."

"I know that." His heart softened. Even with her own issues to deal with, Penny was still offering comfort and support. "I appreciate your offer and thank you, but there's nothing anyone can do. It's going to be a waiting game before this problem's resolved."

"I see." She sighed, stared down at her folded hands.

"How's it going with Molly and her baby?" He couldn't leave her like this.

"She seems a bit depressed since she and her boyfriend had an argument. He keeps asking her to move in with him, and Molly wants her own place. She's determined to get her life on track."

"Is she talking more about the baby?" he wondered.

"She mentioned adoption once." Penny's face tipped up as she met his stare. "I'm really struggling to find a way to help her, Rick."

"You do seem a bit down." Not the most flattering thing to say but Rick needed to get to the point. "Is everything really okay with you? Anything I can pray about?"

"You'd pray for me?" She seemed dumbfounded when he nodded. "That's very kind." Then Penny jumped to her feet as if she regretted saying too much. "But I can't talk right now. I've got to get back to work so someone else can have a break."

"I do, too," he said but he remained in place, unwilling to let her go without trying to help. "Hey, I just had an idea. Do you think Molly would watch the twins if we were to go somewhere after work to have coffee?"

"I guess." She said it slowly, eyes narrowing as she considered his suggestion. "I could ask her."

"If she agrees will you go with me? Please?" Sensing that Penny was about to make an excuse, Rick made it a plea. "I could really use your advice."

"Mine?" Penny blinked, obviously surprised. "Okay, sure. As long as nothing comes up to keep me on the job I'll meet you at your truck at five thirty. I think it's better if we meet there so the twins don't see us and want to come along and then we'll have to refuse them. Right?"

"Sounds like a plan." Rick had no idea what excuse he'd use to solicit her advice. Thankfully he had almost an hour and a half to come up with something, but the topic sure wouldn't be about what was really bothering him because he was pretty sure his sad saga would make Penny back off big-time and that was exactly what he *didn't* want.

It took some doing to wind down the job site on time. When he repeated those instructions his crew kept sneaking looks at him as if they thought he was sick. Well, maybe he was, Rick mused. Sick of wondering what was wrong with Penny because she was his friend and he cared about her.

Just a friend?

Of course. Penny was his friend and he was hers. That was the way they both wanted it.

Rick was five minutes late by the time he got to his truck. Penny wasn't there but she showed up a few minutes later slightly breathless.

"Sorry. Molly needed a break so I had to wait." She climbed into his truck and fastened her seat belt.

Rick studied her tousled hair and wondered if something else had happened. He sensed a hesitancy about her that he was pretty sure hadn't been part of their previous encounters. He had the distinct impression it was because she was hiding something.

"Molly's okay to stay with Katie and Kyle?" he asked.

"Oh, yes. She has my cell number if she needs me and there's another worker with her." Penny glanced around. "Where are we going?"

"Can we pick up a couple of lemonades and drink them in the park? It's cooler under that big Palo Verde tree and we'll get a bit of a breeze from the pond." Rick figured they'd need space and privacy for him to get the answers he needed, and the park seemed exactly the right place to do it.

"Sounds good to me," Penny agreed.

Within ten minutes they had their drinks and were sitting together on a park bench.

"So what is this about?" Penny asked.

"Before I explain, can you answer something?" Rick figured there had to be a way to ask this personal question without offending her. When she nodded, he inhaled and began. "The other night when the twins stayed with you and I phoned, we were talking about kids, remember?"

"You asked me why I didn't have my own," Penny said immediately. Her eyes narrowed as if anticipating what was coming.

"And you said, 'Because I can't.' Ever since then I've been wondering what you meant." There, he'd asked. But since Penny wasn't looking at him he couldn't gauge her response. "I was thinking that if you're nervous about being a mom or something, I'm sure you could talk to my mother. She loves to talk about when Gillian and I were kids and—"

"It's not that." Penny set her paper cup on the grass and folded her hands in her lap. "I can't have children, Rick. I had breast cancer a few years ago and the treatment rendered me unable to be a mom."

Rick gaped, totally stunned by her admission and knowing he showed it. He struggled to find the right words to offer and only came up with, "I'm sorry, Penny."

"Yeah, me, too." She still didn't look at him. "I shouldn't say I can't have them. The doctors said it was extremely unlikely." A fake smile touched her lips. "Actually, that's what broke up my engagement."

"Pardon?" Rick fumed as she told him in a lackluster voice about the jerk who'd dumped her because, through no fault of her own, she couldn't have the kids he wanted.

"His name was Todd. He was a firefighter. I was recovering from a three-year relationship that also ended badly. We became good friends. And then we fell in love." She fell silent, her face sad with memories. Rick wanted to know more so he gently nudged her to continue.

"What happened with the first guy?" He expected her to say *None of your business*. But she only paused for a moment before speaking.

"It's ironic, really." When Penny tipped her face into the sun he thought he'd never seen anyone more lovely. "In the three years we dated I somehow never discovered Jared didn't want children, at all, ever. The night he proposed was also the end of our relationship for me because I couldn't fathom my future without kids."

"Of course not." What kind of dummy didn't know within minutes of meeting Penny that her world revolved around her love of kids? Rick wondered with disgust.

"Todd went to my church and was also recovering from a relationship that had soured. He was there for me all through my surgery, chemotherapy and radiation and somehow in the midst of that horrible time we fell in love. I guess that's why I thought we'd be together forever. I thought we'd gone through the worst life could offer and he'd stuck by me."

The sorrow in her words and the tears glazing her

pretty blue eyes forced Rick to stifle his own emotions and offer consolation. He put his arm around her shoulders and squeezed, a little surprised by how perfectly she fit against his side.

"I'm so sorry, Penny. I had no idea." He breathed in her perfume, soft and sweet, just like Penny herself. "I shouldn't have pressed you for an answer."

"It's okay. I've come to terms with ending that relationship." She heaved a weary sigh. "Todd wasn't part of God's plan for my life. I realize that now."

Penny edged away from him, breaking the close contact that Rick suddenly missed. So great was his feeling of separation that he struggled to focus on her next words.

"Todd was an orphan like me. He'd spent his whole life dreaming of having a family and when I couldn't I guess—well, in hindsight I realize that our breaking up was for the best." Her voice dropped away then picked up the thread a moment later, stronger, more determined. "If we'd married, he would have resented me for denying him his dream."

"Then I guess it's good you found out in time," Rick murmured.

"It is. Marriage between us wouldn't have worked. I know that now. Getting back to full-time teaching, moving to the daycare and working with the twins, all of it is helping me realize that God facilitated my recovery from breast cancer because He has a plan for me."

"Ah. 'The Lord will work out His plan for your life,'" Rick recited thoughtfully, suddenly understanding. "You have that as a bumper sticker."

"Yes, that's my life's verse," Penny said, her gutsy smile appearing again. "It means I can still be used by God only in a different way than I expected." She shrugged. "God has something else in mind for me, I guess."

"But you still want children?" Rick didn't have to ask that because he knew it was true by the way her face changed, got a dreamy look, as she nodded. "So are you thinking adoption?"

"Maybe." She sighed and took another sip. "I'm struggling with that."

"Because?"

"How do I reconcile what I want with what God wants for me when I want a child so badly?" Penny gave him a wry smile. "I'm not sure of my next step." She turned the tables. "What about you? What's happening with these angry phone calls?"

"Angry? That's what the twins said?" When she nodded Rick exhaled. "Guess I haven't been doing a very good job of hiding my work problems from them."

"It's about a job?" she frowned. "But the twins said they heard you talking about their mother."

Penny had entrusted Rick with her private history, bared her heart. How could he do less?

"This isn't easy to talk about," he began. His breath caught as her fingers twined with his.

"I'm listening," she said. Those gently comforting tones drew his confession.

"When Gillian returned from West Africa she was in a lot of pain. She'd lost her husband and she had two small children dependent on her." Rick exhaled, his face and voice tight with tension. "She didn't know what to do and she had nowhere to live."

"So you built her a house." Penny smiled at his surprise. "Well, it's a natural assumption. After all, building is what you do," she said.

"Gill and I, we'd always felt each other's pain. I could see how badly she was struggling to figure out how to go on alone. So I got her involved in house plans. She didn't want much, a safe place for her and the twins, that's all." His nostalgic smile touched her heart.

"A true mom," Penny murmured.

"Then we started construction. One of my workers talked to her about doing a presentation at church and Gillian began to see possibilities for her future. She got involved in fund-raising for a school that was desperately needed in Mali." Penny watched Rick swallow and waited while he paused before continuing. "Gill became herself again with each stage of progression on the house and the fund-raising. Little by little my sister was slowly coming back to us. I had to make her home perfect for her and her twins to share. It was the only way I could find to help her."

Rick's voice wavered. Penny held her breath, waiting for him to break free of his memories and tell her the rest of the story. Because there was more. She could hear it in his words, see it in the flutter of troubled expressions that moved across his face, feel it in the way his shoulders tensed. Her heart went out to him. How horrible to lose your sister in such a terrible way.

"Sorry." He jerked back to reality and tossed her a half smile that was tinged with sorrow. "Daydreaming."

"Nothing wrong with cherishing good memories," Penny said softly. Not that she had any memories of family. She could only imagine how sweet it would be to look back on times of love and laughter with people who'd shared your life and knew you better than anyone else in the world.

"Anyway, my business partner and I worked hard to get that house finished. Gillian was ecstatic the day she and the twins moved in. She'd felt so guilty about bunking with Mom and Dad. The twins were younger then and kept waking at night, which she thought wore out our parents." He shook his head. "Truth was it did but they loved having her and their grandchildren with them. Especially later when—" Rick choked off the rest.

"So they moved into the house you built," Penny nudged after he'd taken some moments to regroup. Again she marveled at the love welling in Rick's voice.

"Yes. Mom and Dad bought a swing set for the twins as a welcome-home gift. I got Gill some new furniture and she sewed all her own curtains. It was a great place, so cozy and warm." Rick glanced at her, his voice soft, oozing pride. "Aside from my parents' place I've never walked into another home and felt so instantly comfortable. Except maybe yours," he added, looking bewildered. "I get the exact same feeling there."

"That's a wonderful compliment and the exact ambience I was going for." Penny's chest swelled with pride. "Thank you."

"You're welcome." Rick's gaze held hers, dark, probing. Prickles of awareness skated up and down Penny's spine but she couldn't break his scrutiny.

It felt as if they connected but it wasn't only because of the electricity zapping between them. Penny felt as if they linked on some deeper, intangible level. Except that in the moment it seemed suddenly too intense and that scared her. She didn't want to get involved again, or more precisely didn't want to get hurt again. So she immediately put up her barriers by avoiding what was happening and instead pressing Rick for answers.

"And then Gillian died in the fire."

"Yes. The house burned fast and hot, incredibly hot." Pain edged Rick's grim voice.

"How did you get there soon enough to save the twins?" she asked curiously.

"I lived a block away. I chose her lot because I figured I'd be nearby if Gill needed me. I happened to be coming home from closing on a job and saw the flames. I called 911 then pushed my way inside. I managed to get the twins out but—" He shook his head, the words unspoken.

"But you were injured and couldn't get to Gillian and she died," Penny finished gently. "Her death wasn't your fault, Rick."

"It could be."

"What do you mean?" Funny how she felt the tiniest bit of fear as she waited for his answer.

"The investigation into that fire has never been closed. Because," he continued, forestalling her question, "they have not been able to ascertain the cause. Ever since the fire the authorities have been focusing on the building to determine the cause."

"They're not now?" she asked and felt a shiver of fear when he shook his head.

"They're now suggesting there was something faulty in the construction of the house, which caused Gillian's death." Rick turned slightly, his dark eyes revealing his inner torture. "I can't shake this feeling that something I did caused Gillian's death and it's eating me up."

"You didn't." Stunned both by his admission and

her own certainty, Penny couldn't find the right words to reassure him.

"The twins are orphans because of me," he rasped.

"No." That much she knew for certain. "You'd never take a shortcut that would cause such terrible repercussions. I know that about you, Rick. I've seen your vigilance in action every morning."

"You don't understand." He raked a hand through his hair, obviously distraught. "There are a thousand things to oversee on a job site. We were hurrying to get Gill into that house, pushing hard. Maybe there was something I missed."

"I don't believe that and neither do you." Penny grasped his arm, determined to help him break free of these guilty feelings. "You know in your heart that you crossed every t and dotted every i."

"That's the thing. I don't *know*." Rick's voice was tight. "I was working so many hours that I usually fell into bed each night." His face looked haggard in the bright sun, the scar standing out like a beacon. "What if I missed—?"

"Stop it. Don't think like that," she ordered but he simply watched her with pity.

"I have to think like that, Penny. I saw my lawyer when I went to Phoenix. Apparently some new investigator they're bringing in is suggesting Gillian's home was improperly wired and that's what caused the fire."

She stared at him aghast.

"They're talking about charges, Penny." Rick's voice dropped to a whisper. "I could go to prison for causing my own sister's death."

Penny sat frozen, unable to console him, even unable to think.

The only thing she *could* do was beg God for help.

Chapter Ten

Penny pulled into Rick's driveway on Saturday evening, still shaken by what he'd told her. His confession had left her feeling unprepared to join him and his family for a happy time.

"Glad you came." Oddly, Rick's warm brown eyes and welcoming smile didn't reassure her.

Was that because she liked the way he slid an arm around her waist to shepherd her inside? Really liked the way he made her feel like part of the family by assigning her a job beside his dad? Maybe she liked Rick too much. Maybe she felt uncomfortable because she was letting him get too close.

All Penny knew was that ever since he'd told her about the fire and his fear that he'd be blamed, a frozen part she'd kept tucked deep inside ever since her breakup with Todd had been thawing a little more every time she saw Rick.

"I'm so glad you came." Eva's smile chased away all doubt about coming. This woman was the most like Penny's image of what her own mother would be, which seemed odd given they'd only met once before and talked on the phone twice. "I've been thinking a lot about you this week, my dear."

"You have?" Penny frowned then wondered if Rick had said something about the confidences she'd shared. She glanced at him and sighed when, as if he read her thoughts, he shook his head.

"When I've had my devotions this week, the Lord seemed to lay thoughts of you on my heart. Is there anything specific I can pray for, Penny?" Eva asked quietly.

"Why don't you two ladies take some punch out to the deck? You can talk in peace there." Rick inclined his head toward the boisterous twins, who were playing a game of snap at the kitchen table.

"But Eva was going to make the garlic bread—" Glancing at his wife, David stopped, shook his head. "Mine's better anyway," he told Penny with a wink. "You two ladies go ahead and leave all the work to us men."

"You should have lots of energy for cooking," Eva teased. "All you did was sit and read on a bench while I shopped."

"Go while the getting's good," he ordered with fake menace, pointing to the French doors that led outside.

"Rick's house isn't huge," Eva said as they walked onto a stone patio with comfy lounge chairs and a black wrought iron table. "But it is perfectly laid out. He took such care to make sure the flow was just right."

"He built this house?" Surprised, Penny looked around. A children's play set occupied a sandy square to the left. To the right lay a small herb garden bordered by some shrubs. Colored plastic children's garden tools stood pushed into the soil. Behind that was a glass enclosure around a shimmering pool. "It's much different than anything else he's done, isn't it?"

"Yes. After his fiancée broke their engagement—" Eva motioned to one of the chairs then sat opposite "—Rick said he wanted a place for the twins that would be their own, a place they could always come back to. A home. He built this place totally with them in mind."

"Very thoughtful." Penny thought of her own longing for roots.

"My son is as committed to the twins as if they were his own kids. In fact, now they *are* his. After her husband died, Gillian named Rick the twins' legal guardian. She'd witnessed how fast life could change, you see, and she wanted to ensure the twins' world would remain rock solid. Gilly always said Rick was as dependable as bedrock." Eva took a moment to regain her composure then forced a smile. "But tell me about you, Penny. What's happening in your world?"

This woman was so open, so loving, that Penny couldn't stop herself from explaining her adoption quandary.

"I want children so badly," she admitted on a huff of relief. It felt wonderful to share her issue with a godly woman she knew would offer her good advice. "But since God didn't give them to me it somehow seems wrong for me to consider adoption."

"I can see why you'd think that but you're forgetting one thing. The nature of God is love," Eva reminded. "He loves us and don't forget, we're His adopted children. Perhaps He's put adoption on your heart because He has a child He's chosen for you to love as no one else could."

"I thought maybe I could adopt Molly's baby," Penny

said then offered a brief explanation of who Molly was. "But now that she's so depressed I don't think it's appropriate to ask about adopting. Anyway, I'm beginning to doubt it will ever happen for me."

"Honey, can I say something?" Eva leaned forward at her nod and held out a hand that Penny grasped, loving the warm connection she felt with Rick's mom. "In my walk with God I'm learning that I can't always anticipate God's plan. For me it always works better if I keep my eyes on Him, keep my focus on loving God. And then when He sends a situation or an issue, I'm able to rest in our relationship knowing that He will lead me through it. Does that help?"

"You mean stop fussing and get on with living and let God worry about working it out," Penny guessed with a grin.

"Basically." Eva's tender smile and the squeeze of her fingers before letting go warmed a chilled part of Penny's heart. Then Katie and Kyle burst through the door and raced across to their play set in the sand. "Ah, here come my sweethearts."

"I thought that was me," David teased as he followed, carrying a huge platter. "Time to grill."

"You're way better at it than I am so I'll let you go ahead, Dad." Rick winked at Penny as he sank into the chair next to her. "While you grill I'll pick your brains."

"Not much there to pick through but go ahead." David flopped the first huge steak on the grill and smiled at the hiss of searing meat. "What's up?"

"I'm thinking of starting a kind of mentoring program for a couple of the kids who come to Wranglers Ranch." Rick shrugged at Penny's surprised stare. "I haven't got a lot of time to spare, but a few of the regular attendees at the ranch are gung-ho about construction. Actually, two show real talent. They just need direction. What do you think?"

"Sounds like a great way to train your future employees." David arranged a variety of vegetables on the upper shelf of the barbecue, closed the lid and turned to face his son. "So what's your concern?"

"It would be a lot of work and I don't want it to impinge on my time with the twins." The uncertainty in Rick's voice touched Penny.

Had either of the men she'd thought herself in love with ever shown such selflessness? She couldn't remember it. Yet Rick, with the responsibility of two kids and a construction company he was managing on his own, was willing to take the time to lend a hand to kids he didn't even know. This was a man to admire.

"It's right to consider the ramifications of your decisions first, before acting," David mused, forehead creased in thought. "It would be ideal if you could work the apprenticeship of these kids into your regular hours, of course."

"That was my thought. But there's the whole insurance issue to consider. And there's bound to be the inevitable mistake and that will take extra time." Rick exhaled. "I can't afford to miss my deadline at Wranglers."

"I doubt Tanner would be upset," Penny offered. "I think he'd be appreciative that you're taking the time to help with his ministry."

"Yes, he's already said that. The problem is I've got another job slated to start immediately after we complete our Wranglers job on September first." Rick gazed at her, a gentle smile tipping the corner of his mouth.

His smile widened at a whoop from the twins as they careened down their slide. "Ah, to be carefree."

"Can you put off the next job?" Penny suggested.

"It's a prestigious project building multifamily community housing that will really help showcase our business name. We've already signed the contract," Rick said. "I can't delay that project without major penalties, which our company just can't afford. Especially not now with Greg out."

"Oh." Penny sank back into her chair, stumped yet amazed at Rick's commitment to reach others. This man wasn't trying to escape responsibility. He was looking for a way to reach out to take on more! And doing it in spite of his personal problems.

"The solution I see is prayer," Eva said, looking toward her husband, who nodded.

"Lots of it. We need to pray that God will work things out for His will." David glanced at Penny. "Will you join us in praying for that?"

"Of course." Penny hadn't expected them to pray immediately but when David started petitioning God, she quickly bowed her head, silently adding her plea for God to make a way for Rick's outreach to kids.

When David finished, Eva added her own prayer.

"And Lord, we ask You to touch Penny, too. Help her to hear Your voice, to rest in You and to wait as You work all things together for good. Bless us now and bless this meal as we enjoy it together. Amen."

Smiling, David rose to check the barbecue. Penny ignored Rick's curious stare to beam at Eva.

"Thank you," she murmured.

"Of course. That's what we do as Christians," Rick's mother responded with a smile as the twins washed their hands under the garden hose. "We pray for one another. Besides, you're family, remember?"

"I'll pray for you and David, too," Penny promised.

"And Rick?" Eva wore a funny expression.

"And Rick and the twins," Penny agreed.

"Good. We can never have too many prayers." Eva patted the chairs on either side of her. "Come on, darlings," she called, her voice light. "I do believe Grandpa has our steaks well burned."

David held up one black-edged piece of meat and everyone laughed. Except Rick.

He stared directly at Penny, his expression thoughtful, as if he'd just realized something he hadn't known before. And then he grinned and it was as if they shared a secret between them.

That was when Penny knew that Jared and Todd, both men she'd believed she truly loved, could never have lived up to her dreams for a husband. What she really wanted was to be loved by a man like Rick, a man who believed in the same things she did—God, home and family.

But she couldn't fall in love with Rick. Especially since he'd given no sign that he was interested in anything more than simple friendship.

Funny, Penny mused. Somehow simple friendship no longer seemed enough.

A week later Rick sat on the beach at his parents' lake, enjoying the freedom of a Saturday off work. Penny and the twins were in the water with Molly, trying amid much laughter and teasing, to teach her to swim.

"I'm glad Penny persuaded Molly to come with you

today," his mother said as she sat down on the beach chair nearest him. "A pregnant mother shouldn't be depressed."

"Your idea to invite her was a good one," he agreed. "And Penny's very determined to get her to relax."

"If anyone can do it, Penny can. She's a wonderful woman, a blessing for the twins and a much-needed help for you. I thank God He sent Penny into our lives." Eva leaned back, her gaze on the water as the twins' laughter carried toward them. "Look at her with the twins. Did you ever see anyone better at mothering?"

"Gillian," he murmured then wished he hadn't when his mom's face tightened with worry.

"How's that going, son?" she asked softly as her hand curved over his in a touch of gentle comfort.

"Nothing new. They're still investigating, but the more they do the worse it looks for me." Rick hated the knot of worry that always formed in his midsection at the mention of his sister. He didn't want his memories of her to always be tinged with darker ones of the fire.

"I thought you mentioned another investigator had been called in?" His mom's pale face revealed her worry in faint lines around her eyes.

"There was some holdup in his arriving to look personally at the site so they sent him the photos that had been taken so he could complete a preliminary study," Rick said, struggling to suppress the bleakness he felt. "Our lawyer says this guy seems convinced that some electrical code violation caused the fire."

"And?"

"It doesn't look good for me, Mom." *Why didn't God do something?*

"But Gillian was your sister. You'd hardly practice

shoddy workmanship on her house." Indignant, Eva's fingers curled in the sand. "Sorry to rant, honey. It just irks me that no one seems able to find the cause of that horrible fire."

Don't upset her, Rick's brain warned.

"Electrical," he said. "That's the stated cause. Beyond that?" Rick shrugged. "Let's forget about it for today," he murmured as Penny and Molly walked toward them with the twins following.

"We came to see if you're going to sit on the beach all day or if you're going swimming," Penny teased, her blue eyes dancing with fun.

"Molly, you look tired. Why don't you and I chat while the rest of them swim," Eva suggested. "Then we'll have lunch."

"Hot dogs?" Kyle guessed.

"No. It's a secret but you'll find out later," Eva promised.

Knowing his mom wanted to use this time to talk to Molly about God, Rick rose and stretched. "I guess I could use some exercise. Anybody want to try the water trikes?"

"Penny an' me against you an' Kyle," Katie challenged.

"Okay. But what does the winner get?" Rick asked, tongue in cheek.

"A kiss." Katie giggled. Her teasing grin surprised him. Apparently Penny, too.

"Uh, I don't think—"

"I'd like a kiss, Katie. It's a deal," Rick agreed before Penny could object any further. He flexed his arms and winked at her. "First one to the buoys wins. Let's get ready, Kyle."

His partner raced to the water and dragged a bright green trike to the edge of the shore, facing across the lake. "Ready, Uncle Rick."

"I am not kissing you, Rick Granger," Penny warned, cheeks flushed, eyes spearing him like daggers.

"So you give up?" He walked to the water, suppressing his laughter at her indignant snort. "Already?"

"Hardly," she sputtered, following him. "But it's not fair—"

"Oh, phooey." His toes touching the water, Rick faced her. "Life's not fair. Don't be a wuss, Penny Stern."

Her eyes narrowed. Her hands smacked onto her hips. She glared at him, obviously outraged. "What did you call me?"

"A wuss. Sourpuss. Grump. Complainer. All of the above." He turned his back on her and walked deeper into the water.

"Really?" she demanded.

"Yeah. Really." Teasing her was so much fun, though Rick quickly lost his grin when he felt two hands on his back, a shove and then his body hit the water. He spluttered upward from the gritty lake bottom with water streaming down his cheeks. "Hey! Not fair."

"Oh, phooey," Penny shot back, laughter in her voice. "Don't be a wuss, Rick."

"Come on, Penny," Katie called. "We can get a head start now."

Rick swiped a hand across his eyes and saw Penny vault onto the trike then begin madly pedaling while urging Katie to do the same.

"I forgot to add cheater," he yelled before climbing in

beside Kyle. "Come on, kid. Pedal. She calls that fair? We'll show her what's fair."

Kyle glanced at him sideways, a frown on his face. When he couldn't keep up with Rick he gave up and planted his feet flat on the floor.

"What're you doing, Kyle? Come on. We've got to win this," he urged but his nephew simply sat with his arms across his chest, refusing to pedal.

Accepting that Penny and Katie were so far ahead they'd never catch up, Rick gave up as well, and faced his nephew. The frown on his face said something was up.

"What's wrong, buddy?"

"I don't want to win." Kyle played with a tassel on the handlebars.

"You don't?" The boy shook his head. "Why not?" Rick asked. *Here we go again with this strange world of parenting.*

"I don't like kissing."

Rick blinked. Well, that was a new one. Now how was he supposed to handle this when he himself actually had a fondness for kissing, provided it was the right person?

"You mean you don't want to kiss Katie and you don't want your sister to kiss you?" That brought thoughts of kissing Penny, which sent Rick's pulse into overdrive.

"That's not what I mean. I don't like kissing." Kyle dipped his hand in the water. "On TV people kiss and then they get mad at each other. I don't want you and Penny to be mad," he mumbled, chin against his chest. "I don't like it when people get mad."

"Not gonna happen, son." Chastened, Rick brushed

his hand over the boy's damp hair. "Penny and I aren't mad. We were just teasing."

"She sounded mad," Kyle insisted. He looked up, his dark eyes troubled. "So did you."

"Then I fooled you, didn't I?" Rick motioned to the pair out by the buoys who were waving at them, big grins on their faces. "Want to head to shore? We could go for a ride in the kayak."

"Yeah." *Now* Kyle began madly pedaling? Rick just shook his head.

Kids were weird.

That was exactly what he said to Penny half an hour later when they were walking along the shore with the twins racing in front, searching for shells.

"The very moment I think I've got this parenting business figured out, they throw me a curveball," he complained. "It's getting scary."

"If they're telling you why they're doing something it's a good thing," she countered, shading her eyes to look at him. "That's exactly what you want to happen. It's when kids don't talk that problems happen. That's when you need to start worrying."

"Boy, thanks for that. Now I have something else to worry about." They came to some rocks so Rick slid his hand over hers to help her. Seemed only natural to leave it there. "Molly's really taken to Mom, hasn't she?"

"Who wouldn't? Eva's a darling." Penny with her floppy sandals couldn't keep up so Rick shortened his stride. "I hope she can help clear up whatever Molly's struggling with. Lately that girl has looked so tired."

"You sound like her mother," he teased then winced at his gaffe. "I mean—"

"I wish I was her mother. I'd coddle her and tell her

a hundred times a day how much I love her and how special she is. I get the feeling no one's ever done that for Molly." Tears welled in Penny's eyes, though she swiftly dashed them away. "I can't even begin to fathom how tough her life is."

"She's got you," he said, squeezing her fingers. "And now Mom, who will shower her with love and try to run her life for her," he added fondly.

"But even better, Eva will give Molly some spiritual direction. That's what I'm most grateful for," Penny said, rather forcefully he thought and wondered why. "Her boyfriend is trying to get her to quit working at Wranglers."

"Really?" Rick frowned. "And do what?"

"Live on the street, I suspect. He hasn't shown up at work recently, has he?" Penny studied his glower then nodded. "That's what I thought. Why didn't you say something before?"

"In the rush of starting Wranglers' apprenticeship program, I sort of forgot about Jeff's lack of attendance." Rick shrugged. "But he isn't your problem. That kid is old enough to figure out that he needs to show up for work. I told him when he started that there couldn't be any skipping."

"I know all that. It's just—"

"Just that you want a happily-ever-after for Molly, right?" Rick grinned at her surprise. "You think I haven't heard those stories you're always telling the kids? Every one of them ends in happily-ever-after."

"Unlike real life," she mumbled.

"Oh, I don't know." He waved a hand around. "This is a pretty good ending to my workweek."

"Mine, too. I'm sorry for being so ungrateful." Penny

squeezed his hand in what he figured was apology. "Coming to the lake is the best break I've had since the last time I was here. I love this place."

"Good. You deserve a break for all you do for everyone else." Rick called the twins and they started walking back to his parents' place. He was fully aware of the moment Penny pulled her hand away. It was right after his mom called them for lunch. Looking chastened she kicked off her sandals and took off running behind the twins as if she needed to get away from him.

It wasn't only kids he didn't understand, Rick decided as he followed. It was women, too. Particularly Penny. But that didn't mean he wasn't going to give figuring her out a good try.

Giving up on a lady like Penny was a dummy move, and Eva Granger hadn't raised her boy to be a dummy.

Chapter Eleven

"I can't stop thinking about the campfire we had at the lake with Rick's parents," Penny told Sophie the following week as she sat in Wranglers' kitchen with coffee and an apple tart. "Especially the stories he told about the family and his childhood."

"Sometimes he talks about Gillian to us," Sophie agreed, pulling another tray of baked goods from the oven. She switched it off and sank into a chair with a sigh. "Whew. It's hot today. I don't know how I'd manage if we didn't have air-conditioning."

"Us, either. The kids are much happier when they're not uncomfortable, especially the babies."

"So did he say anything about his sister?" Sophie asked then sipped her coffee.

"A lot, and everything he said made it sound like they'd been real soul mates." A thought occurred to Penny. "Did you know Gillian?"

"We only met a couple of times. What struck me most about her was how much she leaned on Rick. They were very close."

"That's what I'd guessed from the stories he told

and other things he's said." Penny glanced at the clock and rose. "I've got to get going. Thanks for sharing my coffee break."

"My pleasure." Sophie waved her off.

As Penny walked to the daycare she remembered the twinge of envy she'd felt at the lake over the love the Granger family shared. She recalled, too, how it had increased when David and Eva had included her and Molly in the goodbye hugs they'd shared.

Now, days later, Penny again had that feeling of loneliness, an unsettling sense of isolation, as she thought about her day at the lake. It had seemed to her that she was standing on the outside when she wanted so much to be a real part of the Granger family.

As Penny tried to busy herself filling out time sheets she reasoned that she probably felt left out more acutely now because of Rick's kiss. She hadn't expected it and still remained flabbergasted by it. As it had a zillion time since, her brain replayed the video of those moments.

She'd been helping him load the truck while Molly and his parents got the twins into their pajamas so they'd be ready to climb into bed once they reached home.

Now Penny's fingers lifted to her lips, exactly where Rick's lips had pressed. The same chaotic storm of feelings rushed through her and in a flash she relived those precious moments.

Rick's kiss was no mere brush of the lips, but a sensitive, probing caress that gave as much as it asked. Moments into the embrace his arms enclosed her, drawing her closer, as if he needed her touch as much as she craved his. It had seemed so right to melt against him, to slide her arms up to twine around his neck, to let her fingers curl into his hair and delight in the senses he awakened. His kiss had forced her to face the depth of her own longings to love and be loved.

Even now she could feel Rick's lips pressed against her shoulder, hear the ragged breath he'd inhaled. She'd never felt so utterly content to be in any man's arms as she had in his. Then he'd cupped her face in his hands, brushed her nose with his lips and chuckled.

"I owed you that," he'd said, dark eyes glinting.

"For?" Penny still couldn't get over the way his smile affected her.

"Winning the race. Winner gets a kiss, remember?" Rick's grin said he was laying claim to that title.

"There was no race so no need for a kiss," she said, hoping he wouldn't ask her to forget it. "And even if there had been, you and Kyle weren't even a distant second. Non-compete ribbon maybe."

Completely ignoring that, he'd kissed her again.

"Penny?" A hand squeezed her shoulder. "Penny? Are you awake?"

"Yes, I'm awake. Sorry, Molly. Just daydreaming." She forced herself back to awareness, relieved that two other staff members were watching the children.

"Must have been a very good dream," Molly hinted with a smile. "Care to share?"

"No." Suddenly Penny noted Molly's pain-filled face. "Are you all right?"

"Yes. I stumbled on some roots, that's all." Molly rubbed her side.

"You fell?" Worried, Penny led the girl to a chair. "Sit and catch your breath a minute. Is the baby okay?"

"It's fine. Why does everyone keep asking me that

question?" The cranky tone told Penny that this almost-mom was weary and out of sorts.

"Maybe you should be checked—"

"I am not seeing a doctor," Molly said sharply, cutting her off. "My biggest problem is this kid. He's constantly kicking me. *He's* as strong as a horse. *I'm* the one who can't sleep, can't eat normally and can't get cool."

"I want you to go to the nurse's station, Molly." Penny remained adamant in spite of the girl's angry look. "There's no class on now so there shouldn't be anyone there. You'll be able to lie down and relax there."

"I can't afford—"

"Wranglers Ranch allows their staff to take sick days. You're going to take part of one now so you can get your energy back. But first you're going to eat something. Come with me." Penny led the way to the kitchen area, where two other workers were preparing lunch for the children. "Some soup and a sandwich. I insist," she added when Molly started to object.

"Fine." She flopped down in a chair and studied the soup she'd been served. "What does it matter anyway? This kid will probably end up on the street like me."

"Is that what you want, sweetie?" Penny used her gentlest tone.

"No! But I don't know how I can change anything. My mom sure isn't going to take him." Molly fiddled with her spoon. "I keep thinking about adoption but I'm afraid I wouldn't get any say in the parents or what they did or how the kid grows up."

"I had a friend who gave up a baby for adoption," Penny said gently. "She made several conditions that had to be met before she terminated her rights."

"But that's just it. I don't know what conditions to

ask for and anyway, I don't know if that's what I want to do." Molly set down her spoon as tears rolled down her cheeks. "I'm the mother so it's my job to make sure this kid is well looked after all his life, not just when he's a baby. And I don't know how to make that stuff happen."

"Here." Penny pulled a small notepad out of her pocket and grabbed a pen off a nearby shelf. "Eat your lunch and while you do make notes of all the things you want for your baby. Write down every detail that's important to you."

"Why?" Molly asked with a frown.

"Because then you'll know what to ask prospective parents who want to adopt your baby, if adoption is the route you decide to go." Penny smoothed a hand over her head. "When you've finished go lie down and relax for a while. Why not ask God what He wants you to do? Sometimes when we're quiet is the best time for God to plant an idea in our head. Okay?"

She waited for Molly's nod, complimented the cooks on their work then left, needing a few moments of quiet time for herself to think about the idea growing in her mind.

Could *she* adopt Molly's baby?

It was well past coffee break time so she chose the patio to sit and think further about the idea. But she'd barely begun praying when Rick appeared.

"Hey, Penny. Are you running late today, too?" he said as he filled a glass with lemonade and took the last two doughnuts from under the glass dome covering them.

"No. I came here to think."

"And I'm bothering you. I'll leave." He turned to go but she stopped him.

"Actually, if you don't mind listening, I'd like your opinion on something, Rick." When he nodded and sat down she slowly, hesitatingly, told him her thoughts.

"Adopt Molly's baby." He said it slowly as if he needed time for the words to impress on his mind. "That's taking on a big commitment."

"I've wanted a family my entire life, Rick. This seems like a way I can have my heart's desire. I can offer a child a good home and I know I will love him or her." Penny saw his eyes narrow. "What are you thinking?"

"That it's a huge step to take. Your life won't ever be the same," he warned.

"Good. I don't want the same life. I want a family." She made a face. "I work at Wranglers Ranch so at least daycare won't be an issue for me."

"There's that." Rick calmly munched on his doughnuts without saying anything more.

"You don't think I can do it." Anger lit a fuse inside her. Rick had his loving family yet he begrudged her a child? "You're a single dad," she reminded.

"And I wish every day that I wasn't," he said with emphasis. "Don't look at me like that, Penny. I love the twins, you know that. But I'd do anything for them to have their mother back."

"Why?" she asked, stunned by the intensity in his voice.

"Because I doubt myself a hundred times a day. Would Gill have said that, done that, asked that?" He heaved a sigh. "Being their only parent has meant I've cut almost everything else out of my life because I don't have time for it. I don't begrudge that because I've come to realize that I can only do so much and being a parent to the twins is the most important thing to me. But you're outgoing, gregarious and—"

"You're not going to talk me out of it." Penny glared at him, wishing she'd kept her thoughts to herself.

"Listen." Rick set down his glass, wiped his fingers on a napkin and cupped her chin in his fingers, pressing against it so she had to look at him. "That's not what I was saying. I want you to have everything you've always dreamed of, Penny. Every single thing," he promised very quietly, his gaze riveted on her lips.

"But?" She wanted him to hold her, to reassure her, to—*love her*?

"But I don't want to see you hurt. I don't want to see you ground down by pressures you didn't expect and eventually learn you don't want. I don't want you to take on more than you're prepared for."

Though Penny heard Rick, his words seemed to float past in the truth of what she'd just realized. She loved him. How could she love him? How could that have happened when she'd been determined to escape letting her heart get involved again? She couldn't make sense of it and yet—she loved him.

"Penny? You look funny." Rick's voice broke her trance. "What's wrong?"

He pressed on her chin, forcing her to look at him. That helped her refocus. She couldn't let him guess. She had to hold the knowledge close, think it through.

"I've worked with kids for a while now, Rick." He stared at her as she gathered her scattered thoughts. "I think I can anticipate the problems there will be with adopting a child. But there will be joy, too. And fun and sharing. That's what I want."

He kept hold of her chin, studying her intently with

his dark brown eyes until she had to jerk away lest he see what she'd only just comprehended. But then she had to look at him again and when she did he leaned forward, pressed his lips against hers in a very quick caress then drew away.

"If you're sure that is what you want then I wish you every success." But the words were at odds with the way his brows drew together. "What does Molly say?"

"She doesn't yet know that I want to adopt and please don't tell her. I'll broach the subject when I've thought through the best approach and I'll only do that after I work out some details," she promised, wishing he could be sincerely happy for her.

"I've got to get back to work." Rick put his dishes on the rack then walked back to her, his face absent of its usual smile. "Can I say just one thing more, Penny?"

She didn't want to hear it. She wanted to bask in the warm glow of loving him and of finding a way to have the child she'd longed for. Out of politeness she inclined her head and waited.

"Pray about it. Pray really hard and then listen for an answer. Be certain you know in your heart that this is God's will for you before you talk to Molly. Please?" Then he left, striding away with the confidence of someone who had never known what it was like to question every single decision of her adult life because there'd never been a parent or a sibling to bounce ideas off.

But she loved Rick. What was to come of that?

Hugging the knowledge close, Penny rose and returned to work, the verse she'd memorized on the first of January rolling around through her brain.

The Lord will work out His plan for your life.

In her deepest heart Penny doubted loving Rick was

part of what God wanted, but adopting Molly's baby surely had to be part of His plan, didn't it?

As July turned into August, Rick became increasingly frustrated with the lack of answers from the fire investigation. Living in limbo without knowing exactly what had caused Gillian's death was difficult and he often found himself fighting his short-temperedness. On one of these occasions he saw surprise on his crews' faces. There and then he took a break, the second one of the afternoon, to regroup.

He found Penny sitting on the patio, alone. He almost turned and walked away, would have except she saw him. And he saw tears on her cheeks.

Oh, Lord, his soul cried. *It's bad enough that You don't seem to answer my prayers, but Penny is so sweet. She wants a baby so much. She's lost enough. Please, please...*

"Don't go, Rick." She sniffed and blew her nose. "It's okay. I promise not to bawl all over you."

"If you want to, go right ahead," he offered. "I have broad shoulders." That brought memories of their kiss the other night and he'd been fighting memories of that every time he saw her. Trying to blank his mind of those special moments he retrieved two cups of coffee and carried them to the table where she sat. "Here. Drink some."

"Coffee? In this heat?" she said, one pale eyebrow arched.

"Sometimes the caffeine helps." He sat at the opposite end of her bench to give her plenty of space. "What's wrong?"

"You're always listening to my problems but you

don't talk much about your own. Any news?" she asked before she sipped the strong black brew.

"No. Now stop procrastinating and spill it." He crossed his arms over his chest, waiting, hoping she wasn't going to say what he expected to hear.

"Molly's boyfriend has her convinced that she can sell her baby and make a lot of money. He told her she can ask the prospective parents for whatever she wants because so many couples are desperate to adopt a child." Penny managed a half smile and a shrug. "I don't have fifty thousand dollars, which is what he says she should demand."

"I'd like to have a private word with that kid." Anger boiled inside Rick at the hurt Penny was suffering.

"It's not all his fault." Penny exhaled wearily. "I told Molly to really think about what she wanted for her child and to make a list. She did. Number one on that list is a two-parent family for her baby. There's no way I can fill that stipulation, either, so now I'm out of the running altogether."

"Aw, Penny." Rick couldn't help it. He slid across the bench and put his arm around her shoulders, hugging her against his side. His heart ached for her though from the moment she'd mentioned her idea to adopt he'd feared this might happen. "I'm so sorry."

"Me, too." She sniffed as if her tears were on the very edge, waiting to spill over.

"I guess it wasn't part of God's will." He felt woefully inadequate for offering that pacifier to a woman who'd given so much to him and his family. Penny must have thought so, too, because she pulled away, her sapphire eyes blazing at him.

"You know, that's not much consolation to me right

now," she grumbled. "Obviously it isn't God's will or it would have happened, but where does that leave me? Alone again, that's where." She burst into tears then squeezed her fists against her eyes. "Oh, rats. I'm so sick of bawling."

Gingerly Rick slid closer and hugged her to his side again, offering comfort without words until Penny regained control. What a good sport she was. Yet what a hard life she'd led. The things she faced so stoically— he doubted a lesser woman would keep bravely pressing on.

But Penny did and that was what he so admired about her.

"Okay, enough." She blew her nose, wiped away her tears and forced a smile as she drew away from his embrace. "It's a good thing you came for coffee because I want to ask you something."

"Oh." Rick's angst returned as he tried to fathom handling more than he already had on his plate.

Except—this was Penny, who'd stepped in for him numerous times with the twins. Penny, the one who'd offered to help his shorthanded parents out in their store last Saturday when he hadn't been available because he'd taken the twins to a birthday party. Penny, who'd uncomplainingly held three sleepovers because Rick had to make three more trips to Phoenix.

"Ask away," he said.

"Yesterday Molly told me about two other girls she met who are her age, also pregnant, also living at the shelter, at least part-time. I have an idea to run past you."

Uh-oh.

"I was wondering if any of the cabins have been totally completed."

"Two are ready to go. Several others are almost there. Why?" Rick held his breath waiting.

"I thought they might make temporary homes for these two women and Molly while they wait for their babies to arrive."

For a moment Rick got lost in appreciation for this astonishing woman. In the depths of her own disappointment and sadness Penny still managed to focus on helping someone else. Generous didn't begin to describe her.

"You're a pretty admirable lady, Penny Stern." Could he help kissing her again? About as much as the Arizona sun could help shining.

But a simple touch of the lips wasn't enough for Rick. He wanted more. He wanted—a response from Penny that would soothe this need inside him to be with her, to protect her, to shield her against hard times. Because he cared about her. A lot.

He'd figured that out after he'd kissed her at the lake.

He'd also figured out that it wasn't going to happen.

Easing away, Rick called himself six kinds of fool for getting too close. Penny didn't need more grief and he had nothing to offer her but that. He cared for her dearly, loved her, in fact. But he wasn't going to tell her that nor was he going to let her see how he felt. If the fire investigator charged him he'd have nothing to offer Penny except misery. It wasn't fair to her.

"You'd have to ask Tanner about letting them stay in the cabins," he said quietly.

"I know. But I think he'd agree, if they're ready." Penny's intense stare unnerved Rick so he glanced away from her. "Wranglers Ranch started out as a ministry for street kids so it's not exactly a new idea."

"Then let's go talk to him about it." He needed to put some distance between them, needed to end this yen to hold her, to pretend he had a future, something to give her besides problems.

"Now?" Penny blinked her surprise. "O-okay."

They found Tanner checking the shoes on his miniature ponies in preparation for a riding class for some of the daycare children. He listened to Penny's idea, asked Rick about the cabins and then grinned.

"Fantastic! What an inauguration of our cabins."

"You truly think so?" Penny seemed overjoyed.

"Absolutely. It's another way Wranglers can minister." Tanner went with them to talk to Molly so he could learn a bit more about her homeless friends. "Okay," he said when she'd finished explaining. "Here's the deal. I have some conditions for staying here, but if you and your two friends can meet those, I don't see why all three of you can't use the cabins."

"Really?" Molly looked ecstatic. "That would be fantastic! Lissa and Tara have jobs so they won't be hanging around here during the day." Her face fell a bit. "I will, though I guess I could leave when I'm not working."

"Honey, you're free to leave Wranglers Ranch whenever you like," Penny assured her. "But with the baby coming so soon, you might be wiser to stay on-site."

"Maybe. Anyway, I'll ask the other two and let you know what they say. I'm saying yes." For the first time she seemed to be excited. "Would it be okay if I moved in today?" she asked Tanner. "I have all my stuff with me because I always have to take it from the shelter."

"I have no objection but—" Tanner looked to Rick.

"Give us until five to finish and clean up any debris from the sites around those cabins," Rick said, catching his breath at the joy filling Penny's lovely face. "After that they're all yours."

Molly went back to work, her face bemused as if she couldn't believe her good fortune. Tanner told Rick to put one key inside each building and keep the second key until the job was complete. Then he went back to work, leaving Rick and Penny alone.

Ecstatic, she grinned at him, threw her arms around his neck and kissed his scarred cheek.

"Thank you, Rick," she whispered. "Thank you for building such wonderful places for them to bring their babies."

Rick said nothing. He just hung on, content to hold Penny, the woman he loved with all his heart.

Maybe, just maybe...

"Your phone's ringing." Penny released him and stepped away. "I think you've got a text."

Rick pulled out his phone, glanced at the message and almost gagged as everything in his world turned gray.

"Rick?" Penny tugged at his arm. "You're white as a sheet. What's wrong?"

"The arson investigator is still not able to be here in Tucson, but his investigation has proceeded based on photos of the scene forwarded to him." He stopped, unable to continue.

"But that's good. He'll finally figure out the real cause and you'll be exonerated," Penny sounded excited until she noticed his expression. "Won't he?"

"I doubt it because he's sending my lawyer a new list

of questions though I've already answered everything two or three times." Rick tried to swallow and couldn't. "I don't know if I can go through it all again, Penny," he said in a ragged whisper. "To think of her dying like that, alone and in pain—it's so hard."

Penny gazed at him, her blue eyes stark with the same agony that tore him up inside. He knew from her expression that she understood what he meant, that once again he'd have to relive the horror of knowing exactly how Gillian died. Penny wrapped her arms around him and held on, trying to reassure him when he no longer felt certain of anything.

"We have to pray, Rick," she whispered against his ear. Funny how it felt she belonged here, in his arms. "We have to get your parents praying, too, though I doubt they've ever stopped. We have to ask God to step in."

Rick didn't answer. He couldn't shake the awful feeling that prayer wasn't going to help. It hadn't so far. Certainly his faith no longer had the sense of purpose he'd always treasured. Now it seemed ephemeral, wishy-washy, something he was afraid to trust. God felt distant, concerned with other matters.

Rick was on his own. Just like Penny.

Chapter Twelve

"You threw a wonderful baby shower for Lissa and Tara." A week later Sophie smiled at Penny across the newborn she held. "Besides which, you look great holding that little guy."

"I think caring for five babies pretty well wore out Molly this week but I've loved every moment of cuddling these precious little ones." Reluctantly Penny handed over the now crying baby to his mom.

"Tara and I can't believe all you've done for us," Lissa said, cradling her son.

"No, we can't thank you enough," Tara agreed as she took her daughter from Sophie. "You were there just in time. We didn't know we'd have our babies so close together and we don't know what we'd have done without all these wonderful gifts on top of giving us places to live. I can't imagine how we'd have managed if we had to stay at the shelter."

"Any plans yet?" Sophie asked. "We love having new babies at Wranglers Ranch but I know you were both considering moving home with your families."

"We asked but neither of our parents want us there

now that there's another mouth to feed. I'm hoping to go back to school," Tara said. "You, too, right?" She glanced at Lissa, who nodded. "Molly might join us after her baby comes, which she's hoping will be soon. She's really tired of being pregnant, which I totally understand."

"You're both welcome to stay in the cabins for however long you need, though I realize you'll need to find something more permanent." Sophie glanced at Penny. "We've got feelers out about that so don't give up."

"We won't." Tara grinned. "We're learning that Wranglers Ranch is a place where prayers are answered."

Penny wanted to echo Tara's comment except God still hadn't answered her prayer for Rick's love or sent the child she craved to hold more now than ever. After expressing their thanks once more, the two moms headed for their cabins, babies carefully swaddled against the mountain breeze rippling through the valley. Sophie helped Penny clean up the daycare, where they'd held the evening shower, which many ladies from the church had attended along with some ranch staff.

"I'm a bit scared for them," Penny admitted. "New babies, no home, no one to watch over them, no futures. Do you think we could care for the babies here in our daycare if the girls do return to school in September?"

"Why not? It would probably help their cause with the authorities if they have childcare in place." Sophie frowned. "But what about you, Penny? Is it going to be too much for you?"

"I love kids and two new babies at Wranglers Ranch Day Care is a blessing." Penny refused to allow herself to ask God again why she couldn't have her own child to love.

The Lord will work out His plan for your life, she mentally reminded herself.

"Okay, but if it gets too much, just say the word. Now, I'd better get home. Thank you so much for showering Lissa and Tara with love." Sophie hugged Penny then held her at arm's length. "I don't think I've ever known anyone with a heart like yours. You keep on giving in spite of everything. Tanner and I are truly blessed to have you on our staff."

"I'm the one who's blessed. Now go see to your own baby or Tanner will bring Carter here and wake up Katie and Kyle." Penny peeked into the nap room, saw the twins were still sound asleep on the cots and gingerly closed the door. "Rick should be here soon to pick them up."

"I hope so. You need a break." Sophie headed for the door. "Good night, Penny."

Penny waved her out then finished straightening. She'd begun laying out supplies for tomorrow when the door opened. Rick's dark head peered around the corner. He heaved a sigh of relief when he didn't see anyone then stepped inside.

"Hi, there." Penny tried to control her racing heart but she couldn't stop her ear-to-ear smile.

"Hi, yourself." He glanced around. "The baby shower's over?"

"Yes, and it was so much fun." She couldn't look at him in case he saw how much she wanted to run into his arms and be held by him. "The twins were great, Rick. They're sleeping but I don't think they'll stir much."

"Penny."

Something in Rick's voice—the ragged edge? The desperation? Something made her turn and study him.

His face was a ghastly gray. His eyes had lost their sparkle. His mouth didn't smile. Even his scar looked angry.

"Will you marry me, Penny?"

Her soul gave a leap of joy. She opened her mouth to yell *yes* before realizing that this was not a proposal of love. Something was terribly wrong.

"I think you'd better tell me what's happened. Come outside where we won't disturb the kids. I'll take the monitor so I can hear them if they waken." Penny's worry ramped up when Rick mutely followed her without objection. Her heart sent a prayer for help as she indicated the wooden bench outside the door. "Now, sit down and tell me what happened."

It took a few minutes before he could speak calmly.

"My lawyer is an old friend and today he wanted to warn me that because of the fire investigator's preliminary report, it's almost a certainty that I'll soon be charged with negligence causing Gillian's death." Rick's brown eyes looked empty and hopeless as they met hers. "According to him I need to get my affairs in order."

"I see." Penny swallowed hard. Rick didn't love her. He didn't want her by his side as they strove to reach for a happily-ever-after. He was in trouble and he needed her help. This proposal was a business offer.

"I have to be sure the twins are looked after, Penny."

"Your parents?" she murmured dully. God still hadn't answered either of them. *Why?* her heart pleaded.

"I can't." He sighed. "I guess I never told you that my mother has a weak heart. Dad and I have been trying to slow her down for ages. That's why Gill asked me to be Katie and Kyle's guardian after her husband died. She knew Mom would want to do it but that it would play her out. We've been trying to protect her for years. I can't imagine what this will do to her." Rick picked up Penny's hand and held it as if it was his lifeline.

"She's strong. So is her faith." *Unlike mine.*

"Will you marry me, Penny, and adopt the kids so that if I do go to prison they will be safe in a home with someone who loves them?"

"There's no way you'll go to prison—" Penny stopped because his face was frozen in a mask of utter despair. "What aren't you telling me, Rick?"

"My lawyer has a lot of friends here. He found out through them that Tucson has had a rash of fires recently and that they've cost a bundle in emergency services. With the unsolved situation at Gillian's…" He let go of her hand, raked his own through his hair and continued, his voice ragged. "He believes they're very eager to make an example of the bad contractor."

"But you've been building for years. You've never had a problem before. Have you?" she asked warily when he sighed.

"Remember the house I finished before I started the cabins at Wranglers Ranch?"

"I remember. A lovely place." She nodded, tensing in preparation for whatever Rick was about to say.

"They had an electrical fire two nights ago. No one was hurt, thankfully, but it doesn't look good for me, Penny." Rick's tortured voice scraped across her raw nerves.

Her heart screamed *No!* at God. How could He let this happen to such a wonderful man?

"So we're back to my question—will you marry me? And adopt the twins. I know you'll be the mother they need." He smiled and the tiniest spark of hope lit his eyes. "You've already been like a mother to them. Your heart is full of giving, Penny."

"Yes, but—"

"I trust you because you don't give up and you don't give in. You expect the best of everyone and you do your best to give it right back to them." He touched her cheek. "That's why I want you to take on the twins' guardianship."

"You're very sweet," she whispered, deeply moved by his tribute.

"I'm truthful. You live your faith the way I've always wanted to and never quite managed. I know you'll tell me to keep trusting God, that He'll see me through this and maybe sometime down the road I'll be able to do that," he rasped. "But right now I can't rely on trust. I need your help. I trust *you* with the twins and I know you'll watch out for my parents, too."

"I don't know what to say." But she knew what she *wanted* to say.

"This isn't the kind of marriage you wanted," Rick continued. "I know that. I'm sure you've dreamed of a loving marriage and especially of raising your own kids, adopted or not. But Katie and Kyle will be yours. You're the only one I'd entrust them to, Penny. You'll have your family. It's just that I won't be there."

Rick was right. It wouldn't be the marriage Penny had always dreamed of. Her heart ached at the lack of love in his proposal. She loved this man more than she'd ever loved anyone, more than she'd thought herself capable of loving. She wanted everything that went with romantic love including a partner with whom she could share the intimacy of marriage and the difficulties life brought. She wanted someone who shared her faith. Rick was struggling with that. She'd have to be the strong one, the one who encouraged him to keep trusting God and if he went to prison...

Penny sat next to Rick, silently weighing the pros and cons, trying to sort through everything rationally but vitally aware that he was only asking for her help because he had no one else to turn to. Could she marry him knowing that? Should she?

Penny loved Rick. That wasn't going to change. She loved the way he cared for the twins, always putting them first, always striving to ensure they knew he would never leave them. Yet he was being forced to do just that.

Penny couldn't abandon this man now, when he needed her so desperately. Doing that would shred her heart and soul because she loved him too much. If he couldn't love her back she'd somehow learn to deal with that. But in the meantime she would be there for him, be the rock he needed for the twins, even though it meant she would be a mom in name only.

"Penny?" He sounded tentative and a little bit scared. "You aren't saying anything. Is it too much to ask?"

"No, Rick." One truth shone bright and clear. She loved him. She'd claimed she trusted God. Well, now it was time to trust Him completely. "It's not too much. You know I love the twins. I'd do anything to keep them safe and happy." She took a deep breath. Then, quashing her misgivings, Penny smiled at him and said, "Yes, Rick, I will marry you. As soon as you want."

"Thank you." The words were a whisper Penny barely heard because a moment later Rick was kissing her exactly the way she'd always dreamed of being kissed, as if he needed her to complete his world, as if she was the most precious person in his life.

His lips, warm and seeking, asked for a response that Penny couldn't deny. Her arms slid around his neck and she drew him closer, answering his unasked questions as best she could.

For better or for worse she loved him.

Somehow make it work, Lord, she prayed before giving herself to the joy of his embrace.

You shouldn't be kissing her. Your marriage isn't for real. It's for expediency.

Rick drew back but kept his arms around Penny, nestled her head against his shoulder and tried to organize his thoughts.

He hated asking her to marry him. Not because he didn't love her. Rick loved Penny deeply and completely. That knowledge wasn't new. She was the only woman whom he'd ever felt utterly comfortable about trusting. She was the only woman he could imagine leaving the twins with and she was the only woman he could imagine growing old beside.

But he wasn't going to tell her that. No way did he want Penny to feel she owed him anything. She was getting at least as lousy a deal with him as she had with the fiancé who'd dumped her.

If only he could tell her the truth, make it a real marriage.

No. Not gonna happen. Because if he was sent to prison—better to spare Penny all of that.

"It's going to be okay, Rick."

Her whisper drew him back to the present, to the fact that they were in each other's arms outside the daycare where anyone on the grounds could see them, spread gossip, maybe wreck her reputation. Gently he set Penny free, easing away from her tender touch.

"How do you know it will?" He struggled to suppress his skepticism.

"God's on our side. I trust Him to work out His plans for our lives, Rick." She eased her head from under his chin and tipped back to study him. "God won't let you go to prison for something you didn't do."

"I'm not so sure," he admitted very quietly, ashamed of the words yet needing to be truthful with this woman, who'd offered him only honesty. "I've never really had the kind of rock-solid faith that Gillian had. She was always confident God loved her and she was fearless about charging ahead. Even after her husband died, she seemed to have no issues about being on the right path." He allowed a half smile of memory to curve his lips.

"I wish I'd known her."

"Me, too." Rick knew Gillian would have loved Penny. "She was all gung-ho about her new idea to serve God."

"And then she died," Penny finished when he didn't.

"Yes." He sighed then acknowledged, "That's when the distance in my relationship with God seemed to grow. I can't understand why she had to die. If anyone should have died, it should have been me. I don't have two little kids who need their mom. Gill's death seems so pointless."

"There is a reason, Rick. You just don't know it yet."

"And probably never will. That's what bugs me. Her vibrant dedicated life, snuffed out. Because of me?" He quickly shook off the doubts. "No point in dwelling on it now. If you don't mind, I'd like to get started on adoption papers immediately."

"That's fine with me. But Rick, nobody can prepare for every eventuality." Penny's blue eyes grew dark with conviction. "That's where trust comes in."

He couldn't respond without sounding very negative so he kept quiet.

After a moment Penny asked, "When will we be married?"

"A week from Saturday?" On the lonely drive back from Phoenix he'd thought through every step he needed to take to make the twins secure.

"At the church?" Penny's eyes widened with surprise when Rick shook his head.

"I thought maybe we could get married here. A private ceremony, just us, my parents, the twins, Tanner and Sophie and whomever you want to invite." He waited, hoping she'd agree.

"You don't want a church ceremony? Why?" she asked when he said no.

"Several reasons," he said. "Primarily time. It's going to be tight. I have three cabins to finish by the end of the month. I'm not going to leave Tanner disappointed and I won't leave an issue for my business partner to handle when he comes back to work. I want everything nailed down, taken care of, in case…" He couldn't finish it.

"In case you can't be here anymore," Penny said and nodded. "Okay, we'll ask the pastor and Tanner if we can have the ceremony here."

Rick waited, sensing she had something else to say. Sure enough, a moment later Penny cupped his cheeks and turned his face toward hers, peering directly into his eyes.

"I promise I'll do my very best for the twins. I'll do whatever it takes to minimize the impact on them if you have to—go away. I won't betray your trust in me."

"I know tha—" Her finger pressed against his lips, stopping the words.

"But I have to tell you that I don't believe you're going to prison. I believe God will intercede. What happens then, Rick?"

Penny's sober question forced him to think it through.

"If I am somehow exonerated before we get married, you're free. I won't ask anything more of you. But I very much doubt that's going to happen," he said.

"And later? What if it's resolved later?" Penny whispered, still staring at him.

"Then we'll talk about it and decide together what we want to do." Rick had to hope that would be enough because he had nothing else to offer her. He didn't dare tell her he wanted more than anything to make it a real marriage, that he loved her and wanted to spend the rest of their days loving each other and raising the twins. "Okay?"

He desperately hoped Penny would say yes because he had no other solution.

"Very okay," she agreed. "But, Rick, could we pray first, before we tell anyone else?"

He hadn't expected that but he should have. Penny wasn't shy about her faith or her determination to focus on God's plan. She certainly wasn't about to forget Him when she was making a decision this large. He nodded.

"Thank You, God, for Rick and Katie and Kyle. Thank You for bringing them into my life. Please guide us as we make this decision to become a family. Keep us focused on You and help us to trust You to lead Rick out of this desperate situation," Penny murmured, face uplifted to the spear of moonlight that filtered through the trees. "We're scared and uncertain and confused about the future but we know that You work all things together for Your good. So we ask You to bless us. Make us into a family who loves and serves You. Amen."

Rick added his own amen, but nothing more. After all, what else was there to say? The future was in God's hands. He didn't have much hope God would intervene but Penny did. He'd hang on to her faith and hope she didn't come to regret her decision to marry him.

Deep in thought Rick was startled back to reality when she rose and said, "It's time to get the twins to bed."

"When should I tell them?" he said, suddenly overwhelmed by the details to be accomplished before their marriage.

"We'll do it together over a dinner." She shook her head when he frowned. "I know you have the cabins to finish but we have to get this off on the right foot. Katie and Kyle have to feel included, not as if we decided and then told them how it's going to be."

"Very practical." He stood gazing at her lovely face. "That's just one of many reasons why I'm glad you agreed to marry me."

"Well, you may yet regret that decision," she said pertly. A sparkle of something he couldn't decipher filled her eyes. "Because I'm going to ask you for a wedding present, Rick. But you only have to give it to me after God works things out about Gillian's fire."

"Then I'm not sure you'll ever get it."

"Oh, yes, I will." She clapped her hands on her hips and stared him down. "When God provides a solution,

I want your promise that you'll have plastic surgery and get that scar treated."

Rick lifted a hand to his face, surprised that she'd said it. "I'm sorry," he said quietly. "I know it's really ugly and—"

"That has nothing to do with my request."

"Then why?" Confused and a little hurt by her words, Rick tried to maintain a blank look.

"When God solves the issue of Gillian's fire, I want you to promise you'll have surgery on the scars as a sign that you are finally letting go of the guilt you've carried for way too long." Penny's voice gentled. Her hand slid over his, tender, comforting. "You were not responsible, Rick. You don't need to bear that anymore. You'll see."

That was what he loved about Penny. She couldn't help being so positive and she always spread it around. He leaned forward and brushed his lips against hers.

"Thank you," he murmured, wishing he could hold her for evermore. Unfortunately, he didn't share her faith in God's resolution of his woes.

"Let's get the kids." She'd barely opened the door when Tara came racing toward her, yelling her name. "What's wrong?"

"Molly's in labor," Tara said. "Can you help?"

"Yes, of course." Penny pulled out her phone and began dialing even as she spoke to Rick. "You can get the twins and take them home without me, can't you?"

"Yes." He grinned at her relief. "Go and help guide another little life into this world and know that I think you're an amazing woman, Penny Stern." He leaned toward her and whispered in her ear. "By next Saturday you'll be Penny Granger."

She blinked at him in startled surprise before Tara tugged on her arm, drawing her away.

Rick watched her leave. A feather of peace settled his restless heart. With Penny's help the twins would be cared for no matter what. At least he had one answer to prayer.

Chapter Thirteen

"Happy birthday, Penny!"

Rick knew from the shocked look on her face that she'd forgotten the date. But he hadn't and he intended to make this day as special as she was.

Telling the twins about their marriage last night had been a simple affair, made easier by Penny's repeated assurances that she would still take care of them at the daycare, still love them. She was an incredible woman and she'd agreed to marry him!

"Aren't you ready for breakfast?" Katie asked, eyes wide as she took in Penny's disheveled state.

"Did you just get out of bed?" Kyle asked, obviously shocked by the thought. "We've been up for a long time."

"So have I." His fiancée's glower made Rick hide his grin. "I was having my coffee on the back patio and relaxing since I don't have to work today."

"And now we're here to disturb that." He smiled. "Sorry."

"No, you're not," she said in a disgruntled tone. "It will take me forever to get ready," she warned darkly.

"Better not. We have reservations in—" Rick checked his watch. "Twenty-five minutes."

"Reservations where?" she demanded but the kids prevailed.

"C'mon, Penny. We're starved." Katie tugged on her hand. "I'll help you get dressed."

"Help her fast," Kyle ordered. "'Cause my stomach's growling."

Rick sat down in the chair on her front porch, content to wait. Penny was worth waiting for.

Turned out he didn't have long to wait. Penny's mussed hair was a bit damp and a few drops of water glistened on arms revealed by his favorite yellow sundress, but she made it out the front door in ten minutes flat.

"Thank you for your help, Katie." Rick grinned at his niece. "I owe you one."

He got them all in his newly washed truck then drove to one of Tucson's top-rated hotels where breakfast on Saturday morning was a luxury made for birthday celebrations.

"Can we have whatever we want?" Kyle asked in disbelief.

"Yes. Just don't make yourselves sick. We've got a full day ahead." He sipped his heavily creamed coffee and waited for Penny to recover from her shock. "We're going to be a family soon so the kids and I thought we should celebrate your birthday as a family."

"I see. Doing what?" She pretended to pout when he wouldn't explain.

"What would you like to eat?" Rick asked her.

"Crepes with fresh strawberries and whipped cream.

And bacon. Please." She smiled when Katie ordered the same thing.

After he and Kyle had given their orders Rick leaned back, delighted with himself when the waiter, as per earlier instructions, brought Penny a single crepe rolled and draped across a silver platter.

"One?" She glanced at him, frowned then fiddled with the crepe.

"There's something in it," Kyle noted. "Better unroll it."

Penny did, cheeks flaming with color. But a huge smile appeared on her face as she lifted out a diamond ring. "It's lovely," she whispered, holding the platinum band between two fingertips.

"It's your *marry me* ring from Uncle Rick," Katie squealed excitedly. "He has to put it on your finger."

Penny was sacrificing so much for him. Rick was determined to make this marriage come as close to her dreams as he could. So he rose from his chair, walked to hers and knelt.

"Will you marry me, Penny?" he asked quietly, fully aware that every eye in the place was on him.

"I already said yes," she hissed, dragging out the *s*. When he ignored her, she ordered, "Get up!"

But he took his time sliding the ring onto her finger, savoring the pleasure in her blue-eyed gaze after he rose and kissed her on the lips.

"Thank you, Penny. I hope you won't regret your decision," he said very quietly before returning to his seat.

"Another incident like that and I well might," she shot back, pretending anger though her shining eyes told another story. "I don't like being the center of attention."

"Tough because today you are, birthday girl." He grinned at her. "Shall we eat now?"

It was a happy, lighthearted meal full of laughter and teasing that helped chase away the gloomy tenseness of the past few weeks. And when they were walking back to the truck, Penny's hand slid into his. She leaned her head on his shoulder for a moment before whispering a soft thank-you.

"You ain't seen nothin' yet," he shot back and brushed her nose with his lips.

She was so easy to kiss.

"Where to now, Uncle Rick?" Kyle wanted to know.

"We're going to see the butterflies at the botanical garden." He'd questioned Sophie extensively and learned this was Penny's favorite place.

Once inside the butterfly house, Rick became entranced by Penny's demeanor as the butterflies continued to settle on her shoulders, hands and arms. Katie, though she tried desperately, couldn't get them to do more than hover, and Kyle was hopeless.

"They're such innocent, delicate things. They remind me of the preciousness of life," Penny told him and he saw a tear drop from the ends of her lashes. "So lovely."

They toured the rest of the garden before Rick said it was time to leave for the next surprise. He'd barely driven five miles when Katie squealed.

"We're goin' to Gramma and Grampa's."

"Yes, we are. They want to wish Penny happy birthday, too." Rick saw trepidation on her face and hurried to erase it. "I'm pretty sure there won't be any blue birthday cake for you," he said in his drollest voice.

"I happen to love blue birthday cake," she said stoically.

When they arrived, Eva wrapped her in a warm hug.

"I'm so glad you're here to share your special day with us." Suddenly she grabbed Penny's hand. "David, look at this! It's gorgeous."

"We're getting married in one week. Hope you'll be there. It will be just family and a few friends at Wranglers Ranch." Rick knew his parents understood by the way they glanced at each other before offering him their congratulations.

Later, when he and his father were sitting outside with their lemonade, his father asked, "Are you sure about this, son?"

"Yes. Penny's perfect," he answered, quelling the tiniest doubt that sometimes bubbled inside.

"Perfect for you or perfect for the twins?" David said, looking troubled.

"Perfect for all of us. She's a wonderful woman, Dad. She loves the twins and she'll be there for them if—you know what? I don't want to go there today. This is supposed to be a celebration."

But when he was about to enter the kitchen for more ice, he saw his mom sitting across from Penny. Her voice was quiet and her smile in place but it was very clear she was absolutely serious about whatever she was saying.

"Don't let her back out," he whispered as he wandered down to the lake, confident the twins were happily engaged in making animals with the Play-Doh his mother always kept on hand. "Penny's exactly what we need."

What about what she needed? Was it fair to ask her to enter a sham marriage and care for two kids who weren't her own?

"It's the only way I can do this, God," he murmured.

Me. I. As if I'm the only one that matters.

What about Penny?

Rick knew he'd asked for a lot. But had he asked too much of this woman he'd come to love but couldn't tell her of that love?

Time would tell.

"This has been a birthday to remember. I'm sad the twins couldn't stay up for this part," Penny whispered as she sat beside Rick on the deck of his house later that evening, waiting for the sun to sink behind the craggy mountaintops. "I don't know how to thank you for such a special day, Rick."

"It's been our pleasure." His gravelly voice came from behind her left shoulder. "We're the ones who should be thanking you for everything you're doing for us."

She let that hang for a long time as the questions piled up in her mind. Then, finally, she asked the one question that constantly preyed on her mind.

"Are you sure we're doing the right thing by getting married, Rick?" When he didn't answer she turned her head to see his face. He was staring into the distance, his dark eyes tortured.

"I don't know. But it's the only thing I know to do." He shifted so the porch light shone into her face. "Do you want to call it off? Now, before news spreads all over town?"

"No. It's just—I don't know. Confusing, I guess." Penny sighed as the full weight of her decision returned after a fun-filled day when she'd stopped thinking about what her future held.

"Was it something my mother said?" he asked very quietly.

"Not really, though she very kindly welcomed me to the family." Penny paused but could not suppress the truth. "It's just that we talked about faith and God working in our circumstances and now I feel like such a fraud for not waiting for God to work things out for both of us."

"You shouldn't feel like a fraud, Penny. You haven't done anything wrong. We *are* trusting God," Rick assured her with a squeeze to her hand. "Or at least I'm trying. But God also gave me brains and it would be wrong and irresponsible of me not to be prepared where the twins are concerned when Gillian specifically asked me to do my best for them." His chest heaved as he exhaled. "And truth to tell, we don't know yet exactly how God will work this out so we should be prepared."

"I suppose. Your mom reminded me of the way Old Testament wives were chosen and how they had to be wholly dependent on God," Penny mused. "I sort of feel like I'm not being strong and trusting to the same extent."

"Do you want to call things off?" he asked.

This was her chance to back out, to shake off the doubts and walk away. To quiet that accusing voice in her head that continually questioned the faith she talked of.

And yet here she was in Rick's arms, exactly where she wanted to be. Okay, he didn't love her the way she wanted, but she loved him and being near him, helping him with the twins. This was what she wanted.

"Penny?" His breath brushed her ear in a caress that

sent shudders to her heart. If only God could somehow make it that Rick loved her, life would be perfect.

The Lord will work out His plan for your life.

Okay, then.

"I'm not calling anything off unless you want to, Rick. Do you?" She twisted to get a clear look at his face. Their gazes met and locked. Rick's was clear and determined. He shook his head once. "Okay, then, we'll wait for God to work out His plan."

"Thank you, Penny."

"Don't thank me. We're partners in this." Having made her decision, Penny leaned against her fiancé's chest, his hand firmly wrapped over hers as they watched the sunset.

Fiancé. What a lovely word.

Three days before her wedding Penny felt as if she was dancing at the edge of happily-ever-after, except when bouts of pure joy interspersed with shock and surprise kept her on edge, minimizing her bliss. Maybe it was because their news had spread and everyone kept congratulating her and Rick on their love.

They'd agreed to maintain the illusion of a love match fearing that doing otherwise might somehow stop their expedited adoption process. Since Rick was the twins' legal guardian and he'd named Penny as joint guardian, his lawyer tried to reassure them that there should not be any difficulties with adoption.

It seemed Penny was finally getting her wish for a family, but late at night, alone, she often wondered at what cost.

The sparkling diamond on her ring finger mocked her hasty engagement to a man who didn't love her yet also filled her with pride. Rick was a wonderful, generous, kind and special man. She couldn't imagine marrying anyone else. But lurking under her joy was the question of God's intervention. When would this tense situation break? When would He help?

Molly's brand-new baby boy reignited Penny's desire for her own child but that came second to her longing for Rick to be free of all accusations. Though her arms ached fiercely after cuddling Molly's new son in the hospital, Penny stuck by the promise she'd made to God.

"It doesn't matter about me not having a child. I'll have the twins and that will be wonderful. But it really matters about Rick," she'd prayed desperately and repeatedly. "Please intercede. The only way he'll ever forgive himself for not saving Gillian is if You prove he was not responsible for that fire."

Desperation had also brought out truth.

"I love him. I can't watch him suffer so deeply for something I know he's not guilty of. Please, Father, help. I promise I will never again ask You for a child or a family if You will please clear up the fire investigation."

It didn't seem God was keeping His side of the bargain, though, because on Wednesday Rick received a summons to attend an arson hearing slated for the following week. His lawyer wasn't hopeful since the investigator was now openly placing the blame squarely in Rick's court.

Her only confidante was Sophie and even her best friend didn't know Penny and Rick's wouldn't be a real marriage.

"I thought I'd serve a nice plain relaxed meal for your reception. Tanner says he'll grill steaks and we can have baked potatoes and some salads. Does that sound okay? Penny?"

"It's way too much. Far more than we expected." Penny hugged her and held on until she had her tears firmly under control. "You'll be my matron of honor, right?"

"I'd love to. Do you have a dress?" Sophie asked. They discussed wedding details until late in the afternoon.

Penny had brought a picnic lunch so she and the twins could share supper with Rick before he went back to work on the cabins, doggedly determined to finish them, still certain he would soon be prosecuted.

"Thanks," he murmured when they finished eating, brushing his lips against hers, his arm sliding around her waist in the familiar embrace she'd come to delight in. "I know you're as tired as I am these days."

She hugged him close, relishing the bittersweet contact with him. She loved him so much and she tried hard to remain upbeat and positive. *Help us, God. Please?*

"Go and finish the cabins," she directed when it became too difficult to stay in his arms and not tell him how much she loved him. "We have to make a shopping trip for school clothes."

"I know." He pulled out a credit card. "Charge what you need on this."

Penny didn't argue. Rick didn't need the aggravation. Instead she returned his kiss then watched him walk back to the cabins, shoulders bowed as if he knew his freedom wouldn't last long.

She tried to make the shopping trip fun for the twins, who, as usual, brimmed with questions about the wedding.

"I really like my dress," Katie proclaimed. "An' I like pink lots. Are you gonna wear pink, too, Penny?"

"No, silly. Uncle Rick told us that brides wear white dresses, remember?" Kyle's disgust with his sister quickly passed and they finished shopping early.

Back at Wranglers Penny gave them time to race around the daycare playground and work off excess energy before she got them ready for bed. Three stories later they had drifted off and the last daycare worker had gone home.

Molly stopped by for a visit and quickly handed her baby to Penny to care for as if she was eager to be relieved of the responsibility.

"What's wrong, Molly?" Penny could see the girl was extremely troubled. "Are you unwell?"

"Just tired. Really tired." Molly's face looked ravaged and she was so thin. Penny's heart ached for her. "I'm going to give the baby away," she said at last. Big tears rolled down her cheeks. "I can't keep him. I always knew that, I think. But I still don't know how to figure out who'll be the best parents."

Penny wanted so badly to offer herself and Rick as parents. To adopt this baby and give him a home, to love and care for him, give the twins a brother—she wanted it desperately but she wouldn't make the offer. She couldn't ask Rick to agree to it when he was already crazy worried about the twins and his future.

And on top of that, Penny couldn't get past the thought that perhaps God didn't want her to have the child. If He had, wouldn't he have already made that possible?

But perhaps she could help this needy girl.

"I have a suggestion, Molly, if you want to hear it?"

She waited until she had the girl's full attention then began speaking. "God is your father and He loves you more than any earthly father could. If you ask Him and pray for His leading, I know He will show you the right home for your baby."

Molly frowned. "Are you sure?"

"Yes." Penny nodded. "I'm positive. It might not be right away. You might have to wait awhile and really listen for the answer. But if you ask, I know God will reply."

"Why will He?"

"Because He loves us and He has a plan for our lives. He wants us to lean on Him as we would an earthly father. If we ask, He'll show us little by little what He wants us to do. Then all we have to do is follow it." Katie cried out just then so Penny rose and handed Molly the baby. "Try it," she suggested. "I'd like to pray with you about it sometime, if you'd like that."

"I would." Finally Molly lost the sadness in her eyes. "I really would. Thank you, Penny. I'm going to try asking God. Because I know I can't keep him." She stared down at the child and shook her head. "It isn't right for him. I know that."

"We'll talk tomorrow," Penny called before she hurried inside. As it happened Katie had fallen back asleep. Certain that both children were comfortably resting, Penny returned outside. Since Molly had left she decided to send a few prayers of her own. All of them were for Rick.

"Penny?" The familiar sound of that voice had her jerking her head upright.

"Todd?" She gaped at her former fiancé. "What are you doing here? And why?"

"I'm in town on a case. Before I left, some friends back home told me you're getting married and I—" He seemed at a loss to continue.

Penny couldn't help but recall their last encounter. She was not eager to have this new relationship tarnished with that ugliness.

"Didn't you say it all last time, Todd? That I'm inadequate, that I could never be a mother and therefore never be your wife?" It should have made her feel better to say that and yet Penny felt horrible when he winced at her words.

"I know I was hateful, but please, Penny. Just hear me out," he begged in a voice nothing like she'd heard before. "I came to apologize to you."

"Apologize?" She frowned uncertainly.

"Yes. And to ask your forgiveness. I was a fool and I'm so ashamed of how I acted." He sighed and shoved his hands in his pockets, staring at his feet as he explained. "You might not believe me but what I said—it didn't have a lot to do with you not being able to have kids, Penny."

"How can you say that?"

"Please, will you just listen? I need so badly to say this. It's been eating at me for months." He exhaled. "You see, I'd been having doubts about our getting married for a long while, long before we broke up. But I kept trying to ignore them. Yet the more plans we made, the more my reservations built. I wasn't ready to marry, Penny, and I knew it was because I couldn't be the husband you expected."

So it was still her fault. Penny frowned as anger surged but decided to wait for him to finish.

"I felt inadequate but you seemed so certain about

us. I couldn't face my fears but I couldn't proceed, either, so the only way I could figure to get out of it was to blame you. Actually, I blamed you in order to feel better about myself. It sounds awful and it was." Todd shook his head. "I'm so sorry I did that."

"You're sorry now," she said, lips pursed.

"I was sorry immediately," he corrected. "But it took me a while to admit it to myself and by then you'd disappeared and I couldn't apologize."

"So why bother now?" she asked curiously.

"You always used to talk about God having a plan for us." Todd's cheeks burned. "I never really agreed but I'm starting to."

"Why?"

"Apparently His plan includes sending me here, though I have tried every which way to get out of it." Todd's wry grin confused her. "But I can't run anymore. The guilt I feel is oppressive. I know that's God telling me to make it right. So when I was ordered here on a case, I knew the time had come to face you."

"I don't know what you're talking about. A case?" she repeated.

"Oh, I forgot. You wouldn't know that I changed jobs right after we—uh, over a year ago." Todd stood tall and straight now. "I'm pretty good at what I do, Penny. Besides that, I love my work. I've spent my whole life trying to be the honorable man my father raised, but I can't live with this feeling anymore. I'm very ashamed of how I made you feel when it was not your fault and I knew it. I should have been there for you. Will you please forgive me, Penny?"

How could she have ever thought she loved this man?

Not that Todd wasn't a perfectly nice man. He was. He just wasn't Rick. And her heart belonged to Rick.

"I'm not exactly sure what brought you here but I do forgive you, Todd." Penny smiled at him. "A while ago I came to the same conclusion, that we weren't right for each other. Because God had someone else for me."

Suddenly Penny knew it didn't matter that Rick didn't love her. Because God had a plan, He would work out that plan for her life. All she had to do was trust. And she did.

"Penny?" Rick's voice drew her attention as he walked toward them. "Is anything wrong?"

"Rick, I want to introduce you to a friend of mine from my Seattle days. This is Todd Markham. Todd, my fiancé, Rick Granger."

She didn't understand why Todd's face lost all its color.

"Rick—?" He frowned. "What was the name again?"

"Granger." Rick held out a hand. "Pleased to meet—" He frowned as Todd backed up. "What did I say?"

Todd, ignoring him, shook his head as he gaped at her. "I'm so sorry, Penny. So very sorry."

"Why? What's wrong?" she demanded. "Todd, what's this about?"

"I changed jobs, Penny. I'm an arson investigator now. That's why I'm here, to testify in the case of a house fire that—"

"You're the one who's blaming Rick for his sister's fire." Penny couldn't believe what she was hearing. "It's you who's trying to send him to prison?"

"I didn't know—" Todd reached out a hand toward her, dropped it as he repeated, "I'm sorry. I'm so sorry, Penny."

"You should be. You tried to wreck my life once and now you're determined to do it again, only this time you're hurting a man who would never do what you're accusing him of doing to his own sister." Furious, she ordered, "Just leave, Todd. Go away and don't come back to ruin my life a third time."

Unable to control her tears of anger, disappointment and frustration, Penny threw herself into Rick's arms and wept.

How could God do it? She'd bragged to Rick a hundred times about trusting God. How could He betray her?

Rick hung on to Penny as if she was his lifeline. And in fact, she was the only thing that kept alive the flicker of hope that once burrowed deep inside him. But now even Penny and her staunch support couldn't suppress the nugget of guilt he'd carried since the day Gillian had died.

He had to be responsible for her death. Otherwise God would have done something. Not guilty because he'd caused the fire, but maybe guilty because he hadn't saved her. It really didn't matter whether an arson investigator or a court case blamed him or not because in his heart Rick carried the scars for not saving Gillian. The hardest part would be living with it.

And living without Penny.

"It doesn't matter, sweetheart," he soothed, brushing his hand down her back to calm her. "Don't cry like that. It will upset the twins." Rick kept murmuring whatever came into his head, trying to console Penny while furious that she should have to suffer because of him. He should never have asked her to give up her world to help him.

But there'd been no alternative. He would keep the sacred trust he'd made to Gillian.

Rick loved Penny for her self-sacrificing love that flowed out over everyone she met. He would have loved sharing the future with her, watching the twins grow. But for some reason only God knew, that wasn't his path.

All Rick could do now was make the best of where God led. And protect Penny. She must never know that he loved her as much as he knew and treasured that she loved him. He savored her love, knew it as surely as he knew his own name. He tucked it against his heart and examined it in the darkest moments when he thought losing her would smother him. For Penny he would keep pretending that God would intervene.

"One more day and the cabins will be finished," Rick whispered, loving the way her silken hair brushed his scarred cheek. No chance now that he'd have to keep his promise about plastic surgery. And yet, if he had the time, he would do it to ease sweet Penny's heart.

"One more day and we'll be married. And then what?" She struggled for control. "For the first time I'm really scared, Rick. What if—"

He put his lips over hers and kissed her the way he so often dreamed about. And when she responded his heart rose in his chest and sang for the love of her. Then he gently drew away, hoping those few moments had been enough to take her thoughts away from the thought of God not coming through for them.

"Let's get married first. Then we'll worry about to-morrow," he murmured.

She stared at him with those trusting blue eyes.

"Deal," she said in her spunkiest tone. "But only if you kiss me again to seal it."

Rick had no problem with that.

Chapter Fourteen

She was getting married today.

Penny floated around her house in a daze, making coffee then forgetting to drink it when she fell into a silly dream about Rick loving her and sharing her happily-ever-after with him and the twins. And then crashing back to earth when she remembered that getting married today had nothing to do with happily-ever-after.

That hurt too much to think about so Penny focused on Molly. She'd wanted so badly to see her again, to hold the baby once more, but early this morning when she'd tried to visit, Molly wasn't in her cabin. In fact, it had been emptied. Mother and child were nowhere to be found.

Penny had wept for the young girl whose innocence had been stolen and for the child she couldn't keep, the one who'd reached in and squeezed Penny's heart only a few moments after he'd been born. How blessed she'd been to attend his birth.

Then the phone rang.

"Good morning." Rick sounded calm, even slightly happy. "Do you have cold feet yet?"

"Why? Do you?" she asked, worrying that he'd call everything off.

"Me have cold feet about marrying the most wonderful woman I've ever met?" Rick scoffed with a laugh. "I'm not that dumb."

"Me, neither." Penny felt warm all over and it had nothing to do with the summer sun shining in the window. Silence hummed between them until he coughed.

"Uh, about this bow thing on the back of Katie's dress."

"Yes?" Penny smiled, imagining big, capable Rick trying to calm a wiggling little girl long enough to tie a proper bow.

"So, uh, is it supposed to be lopsided?" he asked in a hopeful tone.

"Of course. We are going for natural, aren't we?" Penny chuckled at his silence. "Seriously, don't fuss, Rick. I can always retie it if necessary."

"Okay. So I guess I'll see you later," he said quietly. "At Wranglers Ranch."

Penny hesitated. "You're sure you'll be there?"

"Long before you will. Don't make me wait, lady," he ordered, a gruff edge to his voice. "I'm not good at waiting."

"Me, neither." Penny smiled, caught up in imagining a future with this wonderful man. Surely nothing could go wrong. Surely it would all work out; God would work it out. Wouldn't He?

Reality butted in with the ring of her doorbell.

"I have to go," she said. "See you later?"

"Count on it. And Penny?"

"Yes?"

"Um, you might also have to fix Kyle's tie," he warned.

"We'll manage, Rick. By the grace of God, we'll manage all of it." Hoping she sounded more confident than she felt she said goodbye again and hung up just as Sophie peeked her head around the door. "Good morning. You look lovely."

"So will you when you get your dress on, which by the way, I am dying to see. Come on, lady. Move. It's *here comes the bride* time." Sophie followed her into the bedroom and gazed at the dress on the hanger.

"Do you think it will do?" Penny asked, suddenly unsure about her choice of wedding gown.

"Are you kidding? It's spectacular!" Sophie hugged her excitedly. "You'll be the most beautiful bride Wranglers has ever seen."

"I just hope it's okay. It's not exactly a bridal dress, you know," Penny worried. She took off her robe and with Sophie's help slid into the dress, twisting and turning in the mirror, watching as the pristine layers of her delicate organza sundress-turned-bridal-gown fluttered around her legs. "It's probably not in the Wranglers Ranch style, either."

"Our style is 'everybody is always welcome,' and you always will be because you're my best friend," Sophie said loyally. "Rick is a fortunate man to marry such a gorgeous woman with such exquisite taste. That pale lemon tone is perfect for a summer bride. You'll knock his socks off. C'mon. Let's go show him."

Penny was still struggling to suppress the butterflies in her midsection twenty minutes later when Sophie turned into Wranglers Ranch and parked as close as she could get to the rear of the house.

"You've decorated so beautifully." Penny forced back her tears of joy so as not to weep at the sight of fluffy tulle bows tied to trees here and there and big urns spilling bountiful flowers over the sides. "You shouldn't have gone to so much trouble, Sophie."

"I didn't go to any trouble. *We* did it because we love you and Rick and we want you to be happy." Sophie hugged her, careful not to crush Penny's lovely dress. "Now, I'll go first. You follow the rose petals to the patio to get to Rick."

"The kids scattered the petals?" Penny asked.

"Yep. We've all had a part in getting you two married." Sophie waggled her fingers and started walking.

Penny loved that each of those she loved and cherished were part of her wedding day, that it wasn't some cold impersonal ceremony in a justice of the peace's office. Her heart began thumping at the thought of what today and marrying Rick meant to her world. Nothing would ever be the same again. *She* would never be the same.

That's when Penny made her decision.

I will trust You. I won't stop. No matter what. I will trust in You to work out Your plan for my life. Please work out Rick's, too.

Then Penny followed Sophie, sandals tapping against the flagstones. She stopped where Sophie waited with Katie and Kyle, dressed in their wedding finery and dancing from one foot to the other.

"Hi, Penny," they greeted.

"You look really pretty," Kyle said, his eyes huge.

"Thank you. So do you. Well, actually, Kyle looks handsome." She glanced at Katie and found her frowning. "What's wrong, sweetie?"

"Uncle Rick said today's the day we get our fam'ly wish," she said.

"Yes, it is." Penny gulped as her eyes met Rick's.

"Then what's that man doing here? Did you 'vite him, Penny?" Katie said, her eyes dark with suspicion. "He's not fam'ly."

Rick, too, seemed irritated as he strode toward them. Penny turned around and gasped when she saw Todd and a man who wore a sheriff's badge standing at the edge of the patio.

I will trust.

"What does he want now?" Rick asked in a low growl meant only for her ears.

Penny could hardly speak around the fear gripping her. Was Todd here to have Rick arrested before their wedding could take place?

I will trust. She mentally repeated the words.

"Todd?" Gathering her skirts and her courage Penny walked toward him. "This is our wedding day. After your apology I hope you're not here to spoil it. Why are you here?"

"To give you a wedding gift. This is Sheriff Peters. He'll be a witness." Todd smiled at Katie. "Boy, that little one looks as fierce as you, Penny."

"What do you want from us?" It was clear Rick's patience had worn thin.

From the corner of her eye Penny saw Eva and David move closer but her concern lay with Rick. He was tense with fear. She touched his arm then rose on her tiptoes and whispered words meant only for the man she loved.

"Remember the God we serve. He is well able to handle anything. But you have to trust Him, Rick. Totally."

She straightened, slid her arm through his and

waited. She knew the exact moment he decided. A shudder worked through him before he finally nodded.

"I'm trusting God," he murmured then brushed his lips across hers.

"Hey, lovebirds, don't you want to hear about my gift?" Todd asked, smiling when they broke apart. He seemed unnaturally cheery until he glanced at the twins. "Uh, it might be better if they receive a later condensed version."

Rick gestured to Sophie, who shepherded the twins away, much to their disgust.

"Okay. What is this about, Todd?" Penny wrapped her hand in Rick's and hung on.

"I couldn't stand thinking that I'd ruined your life by finding Rick at fault for that fire. It tore me up but I didn't know how to fix it. Then last night when I was on my way back to Phoenix I remembered a previous case I worked on. That sparked another memory that wouldn't go away and it gave me an idea." Todd looked deadly serious now. "So I came back to Tucson, got some helpers and some huge lights and we went to what remains of the house. I'm sure glad they refused to demolish it until a cause was determined."

"And?" Penny's patience was exhausted.

"In the wee hours of the morning I completed a personal and very thorough inspection of everything left over from the fire. Then I compared photos I'd taken there with photos of another case, which I have on my computer."

Todd's pause made Penny grit her teeth with tension. She squeezed Rick's hand tighter and finally prodded, "You found something?"

"I told you I'm good at what I do, Penny." He grinned

then continued. "In my personal inspection of the house I found evidence no one had reported. They probably didn't know to report it but what I saw almost exactly matches something I've noted in two previous fires; a specific fire pattern that is electrically based but is not caused by faulty wiring." He faced Rick. "I must apologize to you. You were unjustly accused. I do not believe you did anything to cause the fire at your sister's home."

Penny could hardly breathe. Rick was free? Innocent?

"Then what did cause it?" Rick demanded but his relief was obvious as he returned the squeeze on Penny's hand.

"I believe I have enough evidence to prove that the fire in your sister's house was due to a faulty electrical breaker. Two other cases had used the identical breakers, and the fires burned in the same way. Hot and fast because the electrical breaker in the box was the conductor. Not faulty wiring or shoddy building practices."

"But we didn't use anything unusual for wiring," Rick argued.

"No. Your electrician used breakers that are perfectly legal. However," Todd continued, "they are also defective. They do not always fully trip. Instead they continue to carry the full load, which causes the fire."

"Then why didn't anyone else notice this?" David demanded.

"Because the breakers do eventually trip, when the fire gets hot enough. By then it's too late but investigators can't see that unless they've seen previous cases that are very similar." Todd nodded at their shocked faces. "I tried my hypothesis in the lab and the result was the same every time. That particular brand of breaker trips *after* the fire has started."

"So what now?" Penny asked because Rick had fallen strangely silent.

"Tomorrow morning I will file my report. My boss will then issue a directive to have that particular breaker removed from all homes in which it has been installed. Fortunately, they've only been in circulation for just under two years. Unfortunately, the problem was not discovered in time to save your sister's life. I'm so very sorry about that."

With a sad smile Todd glanced at the faces around the group. Penny couldn't speak. She was too busy considering the ramifications of what he'd said.

It meant Rick no longer needed her.

That knowledge was devastating. She needed to get away, to leave before she burst into tears at the utter collapse of her hopes and dreams. She tried to ease her fingers free of Rick's but he wouldn't let go.

"Your sister did not die in vain," Todd said to Rick to cover the yawning silence. "If you hadn't pressed your innocence so hard, if Penny hadn't insisted you'd done nothing wrong, if I hadn't felt compelled to take another look at the house so as not to cause Penny any more pain—well, let's just say many more people might have died. You can take some comfort in knowing that your sister's death will save hundreds of lives."

"You mean neither my son nor his company are guilty of any wrongdoing?" David said, his relief obvious.

"Exactly. I apologize for the problems you've had, Rick." Todd smiled. "I doubt you'll have more related to this matter so now you two can go ahead and get married without that hanging over your head. Congratulations."

Penny dragged her hand free of Rick's so she could hug her former fiancé. Todd was a wonderful man but now she felt nothing more than deep friendship toward him. Believing that she loved him—that, too, had been an illusion. Just like her dream of marrying Rick.

"Thank you for persisting, Todd. You can't know how much it means to us."

"I think I do. I'm just glad I could rectify my mistake before it caused more problems. I'll go now and let you two get married, with my best wishes, Penny." He kissed her cheek then quickly left.

"Not guilty," Rick murmured but Penny thought only she heard him say it.

"Well, now what?" Eva asked, glancing from her son to Penny.

"What now?" Tanner shrugged as if it was obvious. "They get married, of course."

"I'm not sure—" Penny frowned when Rick cut her off.

"Can you all give Penny and me a moment? Please? There's something we need to discuss privately. Come on, Penny." Without another word Rick grabbed her hand and pulled her toward the daycare. "If nothing else we should be able to get some privacy in the nursery," he muttered.

But when they stood in that room, with the door closed, he couldn't seem to find the words he needed.

"Congratulations, Rick." Penny dredged up a smile. "It's the best possible news."

"Is it?" He was looking at her in an odd way, as if he hadn't really seen her before.

"Of course. You and your company are blameless—"

"I am not blameless in Gillian's death, Penny." Rick's mouth twisted in a half smile. "I didn't get her out and I should have."

"We've been over this. You know you're not to blame." But he didn't know that. She could see it in the way he looked at her, eyes narrowed. She had to do something. "How long are you going to pay, Rick? What does Gillian's death demand? A lifetime of guilt? Forever berating yourself? Do you think your loving sister would have demanded that of you?"

Rick stared at her, his face darkening with anger. "Now wait a moment—"

"No. Let's get it all said. Tell me when you'll feel you've paid enough for your failure." Penny wanted him to fight—if not for her then for himself and his future. "You were ready to hand the twins over to me and walk away to prison to staunch the guilt you can't get over." She wrenched off her precious engagement ring and held it out. "Well, that option's closed now because I don't intend to stick around and make it easier for you to carry your guilt."

"You're not marrying me?" Rick asked, his voice deceptively mild as he pocketed her ring.

"That's right," she snapped, angry that she'd been so close to having her dream and now it was she who was throwing that precious vision of a family away. "I don't want to marry a man who won't fight for himself, for the life he deserves, for the children who count on him. Guilt takes up too much room in your world, Rick. There's no room for anything else."

"You're wrong." He stood tall in his black suit, his

dark eyes holding hers with their intensity. "There's oodles of room in my world for love."

"For Gillian, yes. But she's gone, Rick," Penny reminded. "And you have to let her go. You have to—"

"Love for you." He walked to her without breaking his stare. "I would gladly go to prison if it meant I got to marry *you*," he said softly, cupping her face in his palms. "*You're* my world, my darling Penny. *You* make things work when no one else can."

She couldn't say a word.

"You're right, my dearest shining Penny. I was hanging on to guilt. I didn't think I deserved anything more. I guess I was afraid. And then you came bursting in and took over my life and all I wanted was you."

"Me?" she squeaked, shocked to her core. "You're saying—you're in love with me?" Disbelief filled her. "But I'm just a means to an end, a way to keep the twins. And now you don't need me anymore, Rick."

She turned, walked toward the door.

"I will always need you, Penny. I need you to keep reminding me that Gillian would have forgiven me so I have to forgive myself." He walked closer. "I'll need you to remind me that trusting God is an active not a passive verb." Another step. "I'll especially need you to help me laugh and tease and share life with the twins the way a father should." He took her hands in his. "Penny, I love you. Don't you know that?"

Actually, she didn't.

"I love your laugh and your joy and your faith and most of all your generous love that you spread everywhere, on everyone. On me." He stepped nearer still, his face mere inches from hers, voice dropping to an intimate whisper. "I love that you willingly, without counting the cost to yourself, stepped in to help with the twins that very first day, and you haven't quit since. You just keep giving, keep on loving. I need you to love me, Penny. Because I love you. I have for a long time."

"I—I don't believe that," she sputtered, afraid to trust in what he said, afraid to trust that this man could be her very own happily-ever-after.

"Too bad, lady, because I do love you. And I can prove it to you." Rick pulled out her engagement ring and held it toward her, his face creased in a wide smile. "Did you ever really look at this ring?"

"For hours," she admitted, unable to look at him out of sheer embarrassment. "I couldn't believe we were going to be a family, that you thought enough of me to give me a diamond ring or that I was worthy of it."

"You are more than worthy, sweetheart. But we'll discuss that later. What I want to know now is, in all those staring hours, did you never see the inscription?" he asked so tenderly she wanted to weep. "Never read it?"

"How could I? I never took it off, not since you put it there. Not till today. So how could I read anything?" She tried to take the ring but he wouldn't let go of it. "What does it say?"

He held it so she had to lean in to read it.

All my love, Rick.

Her gaze flew to his, her question unspoken but needing a response just the same.

"I thought, hoped that one day, when I was sitting in prison and you were fed up with caring for my mess, that you'd take off the ring, see the inscription and decide you couldn't leave just yet. That you might feel something for me." The yearning in his voice reached into her heart. "I hoped you'd stay, that you'd be there waiting and that one day we'd be together. I've hoped an awful lot lately, Penny."

"Do you know what I hoped?" she said when she finally found her voice beneath a rush of tears. He slowly shook his head. "I hoped that once you married me you'd realize you loved me even a tenth of how much I love you. That's all I wanted, Rick. Just a tiny bit of your heart."

"Silly Penny," he said, sliding the ring back on her finger and kissing it in place. Then he wrapped her in his embrace and bent his head. "Silly to be content with so little when you have my whole heart. I love you, darling Penny."

"And I love you, dearest Rick." Penny couldn't believe the promise that was in his kiss. The breathless promise of a future filled with more than she'd ever dared dream about.

"I know you love me, sweetheart," he said very quietly, his face sober. "That and prayer are the only things that have kept me going."

"Oh, Rick." She took a few moments to show him how much he meant to her world.

"Listen," he said, drawing away too soon. "I know this is really short notice, Penny Stern. But you have the most beautiful dress and Katie and Kyle need mothering and I need a wife and—will you please marry me?" Rick smiled into her eyes. "Today. Now?"

"It can't be too soon for me." As they turned to leave the building she slid her hand into his. "God has used this daycare and Wranglers Ranch for so many things. Today He used it to bring us together. It just goes to prove—"

"The Lord will work out His plan for your life," Rick quoted with her and nodded without hesitation. "I finally get it. He's brought us this far. We can trust Him with all our tomorrows."

Arm in arm they hurried back to the patio, where the twins were disheveled and not in a very good mood until Rick whispered something to them. Katie and Kyle hurried over to Penny, took their baskets from Sophie and waited for the signal to walk arm in arm across the patio toward Rick. Then came Sophie followed by Penny, who carried a sheaf of red roses that Eva had given her while whispering, "It's going to be so wonderful to have a daughter again."

Hearts filled to overflowing, the couple pledged their love to each other in front of friends and family with strong voices and loving glances. Finally they were pronounced husband and wife and sealed their promises with a kiss.

"Too long," Katie protested.

"Way too long for kissing," Kyle agreed, his nose wrinkled in distaste.

While everyone else applauded, their wise grandfather suggested they'd better get used to it.

In the beauty of Wranglers Rach with grains of rice scattering all around her and her arm snug in Rick's, Penny felt as if she was walking on air. Her heart brimmed with thanksgiving as the twins then Eva and David hugged her and welcomed her to their family. At last she had the family she'd always longed for.

A few minutes later Sophie invited everyone to gather around the tables loaded with food to celebrate the wedding. Then Tanner proposed a toast.

"To a couple with hearts ready to be used by God.

May He use them mightily, give them a glorious reward and a wonderful future together."

Everyone raised their glass to the smiling bride and her grinning groom. As gentle music filled the place where she'd shared so many happy coffee breaks with Rick, Penny gloried in dancing as his wife, even if he kept whispering teasing things that alternately made her blush or duck her head in embarrassment. As late afternoon turned to evening on the most wonderful day of her life, Penny's cup was full.

"It's time for us to leave on our honeymoon, wife of mine," Rick murmured when the stars began to blink overhead.

"I love that word—I didn't know we're having a honeymoon." Her heart beat so fast she felt giddy. "Where are we going?"

"Phoenix. On Monday morning I'll keep my promise to you, Penny." Rick trailed a fingertip across her cheek to touch her lips then replaced it with his lips.

"What promise?" she asked dreamily sometime later.

"The one to see a plastic surgeon if God came through for us. Monday morning, nine a.m. You and I, Mrs. Granger."

"Rick!" Penny threw her arms around him and hugged him with the joy of knowing that this was a symbol of his faith in God. "But you don't have to do it," she whispered.

"I think I do, my darling. If only for me, to remind me that I don't have all the answers but I know the one who does and He will lead me." He kissed her then urged, "Throw your bouquet so we can leave, please?"

Sophie gathered the small group of ladies who were

present including Lissa and Tara. She handed Penny her roses then turned her around. "Ready?"

"Throw hard, sweetheart," Rick urged.

So Penny heaved the gorgeous bouquet as hard as she could and was gratified by a squeal of surprise. She turned and saw an astonished Molly holding the flowers. After her surprise abated that young woman picked up her baby carrier and hurried toward them.

"Molly! I'm so glad to see you. Are you all right?" Penny examined her face, searching for some hint as to her absence. Instead she marveled at the girl's radiant glow.

"I went away to think and pray like you said I should." Molly's eyes shone. "He spoke to me, Penny. God told me what I should do about my baby."

"I knew He would." In a rush of tenderness Penny gathered her slim hand into her own. "I've been praying you'd hear Him. Do you want to share?"

"I have to." Molly stared into the tiny face of her son for a long moment then held out the carrier. "You and Rick are the perfect choice as parents for my baby."

"Us?" Penny frowned, glancing from Molly to Rick. "You want us to adopt your son?"

"You are the ones God showed me would be the parents he needs," Molly confirmed. "I've watched you both with the twins, at the daycare and with Tara and Lissa and their babies and with Jeff, even though he didn't appreciate your help."

"He'll come around, Molly," Rick said quietly. "He just needs to grow up."

"That's what I told him when I refused to move in with him." Molly giggled at their surprised looks. "I'm not dumb. He's just a friend."

"But about the baby—" Penny was afraid to believe it.

"I know what I'm doing. I've watched you and I've prayed about it," Molly said, her voice strong. "You have the kind of hearts I want my baby to be raised with."

"But, Molly," Penny argued, wanting to be certain. "What about your list, all the things you wanted for your son?"

"You'll give them to him. I know that. That's what I'm trying to tell you. That's why God wants you to raise my baby." Molly took Rick's hand in hers. "The way you made those cabins, with secret hidey-holes and special lights and window seats and then worked so many overtime hours to make sure they were finished on time so that folks could enjoy them—I could see that you love kids. I know you're a wonderful father."

"Oh, he is." Penny couldn't stop her happy tears from overflowing.

"And you, dear, sweet friend." Molly teared up. "I was hurting so bad and you came along, offered me a job, had faith in me and kept encouraging me to press on. When my life was at its darkest you were the light drawing me in. I don't know for sure what God has in my future, but for now I'd like to stay here at Wranglers Ranch working in the daycare."

"With the babies?" Penny asked with a frown. "Still with the babies?"

"Of course. And when you bring your baby I'll care for him, too. Because he *is* your baby, Penny. Yours and Rick's. He belongs with those who will love him and teach him about loving God. You're his family." Molly held out the baby carrier toward them.

Penny's heart sang a song of pure joy. A child, she would have a child, a baby to love and care for and raise to know God. But this couldn't be only her decision. She turned, studied Rick's face, trying to gauge his thoughts as she controlled her overwhelming desire to take the child from Molly. Without Rick her dream could not live.

"Molly, Penny and I would love to raise your baby as our own child." Rick touched her shoulder tenderly, his voice soft. "Penny's always wanted to be a mom and you're making her dearest dream come true. Thank you hardly seems enough."

"Uncle Rick an' Penny an' you an' me an' a baby. We're getting our fam'ly wish," Katie gloated from her hiding place behind a big urn.

"Yeah, we are," Kyle agreed then ordered, "Shh! We're not s'posed to listen to other people's talk, Gramma said."

"Come on, you two eavesdroppers," Rick called with a laugh. "Might as well join us."

The twins scampered out, dirty, disheveled but smiling with pure joy as they admired their new brother. Rick picked up the baby and laid him in Penny's arms then gathered his family in his strong embrace.

Penny couldn't stop smiling. A mom. She was going to be a mom.

Rick suddenly let go of them.

"There's just one problem, Molly. Well, maybe two. First, we want, no we insist, that you be part of his world so this child will always know all his family and that you love him."

"Really? I'd like that. But I promise I won't interfere," Molly whispered as she teared up.

"You're always welcome in our home because now you are a part of our family. Now, about our second problem." Rick grinned at Penny. "We're wondering—could you possibly look after our new son until we return from our honeymoon?"

"I'd love to," Molly began.

"Actually, there's a third problem, Rick." Penny grinned at him. "I was hoping Molly would agree to stay at my house since I won't be needing it anymore because I have a new home. It's a nice place," she told Molly. "And the garden has lots of veggies just begging to be eaten. You'd really be doing me a favor."

"God sure knows what He's doing," Molly blubbered. "Two answers in one day. Wow. Thank you."

A group hug seemed appropriate but it couldn't last long.

"Sweetheart, we've got to go," Rick insisted. He kissed the baby's brow, waited for Penny to do the same before he handed him back to Molly. Then he swept Penny off her feet and into his arms. "Check with Sophie for the key, Molly, and if you need help. She might need your help, too, since she's agreed to watch the twins for us. And take good care of our boy. Katie, Kyle, we love you both very much and we'll see you soon." Then he strode toward his truck with Penny calling goodbye between giggles of pure happiness.

As they drove off Wranglers Ranch toward Phoenix Penny turned to look back. The twins stood on either side of Molly, waving madly. Her family. And her husband.

"The Lord will work out His plan for your life," she repeated. "I wonder how many times and how many ways He's done that for the many people who come to Wranglers Ranch?"

"I wonder, my dear wife, how many ways He'll work out His plan for our future?" Rick said.

"I don't know," Penny said. She hugged his side and smiled. "He's given me a husband, three children, wonderful friends and a job, all of which I love dearly. I can hardly wait to see what's He's included in the rest of His plan."

"Me, neither."

Side by side, with thankful hearts overflowing with love, the newlyweds rode into their future, one they would trust with their heavenly Father.

* * * * *

If you enjoyed this story, pick up the
other WRANGLERS RANCH *books,*

THE RANCHER'S FAMILY WISH
HER CHRISTMAS FAMILY WISH
THE COWBOY'S EASTER FAMILY WISH

and these other stories from Lois Richer:

A DAD FOR HER TWINS
RANCHER DADDY
GIFT-WRAPPED FAMILY
ACCIDENTAL DAD

Available now from Love Inspired!

Find more great reads at www.LoveInspired.com

Dear Reader,

I'm so glad you've made a return visit to Wranglers Ranch. You're always welcome here.

Penny longed to be a mom. What a time she went through to learn that God always has a plan and if we wait on Him, He will lead us. And how poor Rick struggled with his guilt. Guilt can sometimes correct our actions but it's often something we needlessly carry. Katie and Kyle's world was turned upside down and yet for them, too, God had a plan.

I hope you've enjoyed this last story in the Wranglers Ranch series. I hate to leave Tucson. It's one of my favorite places. The beauty and wonder of the desert always amazes me. I'd love to hear from you in any of these ways: snail mail at Box 639, Nipawin, Sk. Canada S0E 1E0; email at loisricher@gmail.com, Facebook at loisricher/author or through my website at www.loisricher.com. I promise to answer as quickly as I can.

Until we meet again, may you rest in the confident knowledge that God has a plan for your life, too.

Blessings,

Lois
Richer

COMING NEXT MONTH FROM
Love Inspired®

Available July 18, 2017

A GROOM FOR RUBY
The Amish Matchmaker • by Emma Miller
Joseph Brenneman is instantly smitten when Ruby Plank stumbles—literally—into his arms. The shy mason sees all the wonderful things she offers the world. But with his mother insisting Ruby isn't good enough, and Ruby keeping a devastating secret, could they ever have a happily-ever-after?

SECOND CHANCE RANCHER
Bluebonnet Springs • by Brenda Minton
Returning to Bluebonnet Springs, Lucy Palermo is determined to reclaim her family ranch and take care of her younger sister. What she never expected was rancher neighbor Dane Scott and his adorable daughter—or that their friendship would have her dreaming of staying in their lives forever.

THE SOLDIER'S SECRET CHILD
Rescue River • by Lee Tobin McClain
Widow Lacey McPherson is ready to embrace the single life—until boy-next-door Vito D'Angelo returns with a foster son in tow. Now she's housing two guests and falling for the ex-soldier. But will the secret he's keeping ruin any chance at a future together?

REUNITING HIS FAMILY
by Jean C. Gordon
Released from prison after a wrongful charge, widowed dad Rhys Maddox wants nothing more than custody of his two sons. Yet volunteering at their former social worker Renee Delacroix's outreach program could give him a chance at more: creating a family.

TEXAS DADDY
Lone Star Legacy • by Jolene Navarro
Adrian De La Cruz is happy to see childhood crush Nikki Bergmann back in town and bonding with his daughter. But he quickly sees the danger of spending time together. With Nikki set on leaving Clear Water, could their wish for a wife and mother ever become reality?

THEIR RANCH REUNION
Rocky Mountain Heroes • by Mindy Obenhaus
Former high school sweethearts Andrew Stephens and Carly Wagner reunite when Andrew's late grandmother leaves them her house. At odds on what to do with the property, when a fire at Carly's inn forces the single mom and her daughter to move in, they begin to agree on one thing: they're meant to be together.

_____

LICNM0717

Get 2 Free Books,
Plus 2 Free Gifts—
just for trying the Reader Service!

Love Inspired®

SPECIAL EXCERPT FROM

Love Inspired®

*Ruby Plank comes to Seven Poplars to find a husband and
soon literally stumbles into the arms of Joseph Brenneman.
But will a secret threaten to keep them apart?*

Read on for a sneak preview of
A GROOM FOR RUBY by **Emma Miller,**
available August 2017 from Love Inspired!

A young woman lay stretched out on a blanket, apparently
lost in a book. But the most startling thing to Joseph was
her hair. The woman's hair wasn't pinned up under a *kapp*
or covered with a scarf. It rippled in a thick, shimmering
mane down the back of her neck and over her shoulders
nearly to her waist.

Joseph's mouth gaped. He clutched the bouquet of
flowers so tightly between his hands that he distinctly heard
several stems snap. He swallowed, unable to stop staring
at her beautiful hair. It was brown, but brown in so many
shades…tawny and russet, the color of shiny acorns in
winter and the hue of ripe wheat. He'd intruded on a private
moment, seen what he shouldn't. He should turn and walk
away. But he couldn't.

"Hello," he stammered. "I'm sorry, I was looking for—"

"Ach!" The young woman rose on one elbow and twisted
to face him. It was Ruby. Her eyes widened in surprise.
"Joseph?"

"*Ya.* It's me."

Ruby sat up, dropping her paperback onto the blanket, pulling her knees up and tucking her feet under her skirt. "I was drying my hair," she said. "I washed it. I still had mud in it from last night."

Joseph grimaced. "Sorry."

"Everyone else went to Byler's store." She blushed. "But I stayed home. To wash my hair. What must you think of me without my *kapp*?"

She had a merry laugh, Joseph thought, a laugh as beautiful as she was. She was regarding him with definite interest. Her eyes were the shade of cinnamon splashed with swirls of chocolate. His mouth went dry.

She smiled encouragingly.

A dozen thoughts tumbled in his mind, but nothing seemed like the right thing to say. "I…I never know what to say to pretty girls," he admitted as he tore his gaze away from hers. "You must think I'm thickheaded." He shuffled his feet. "I'll come back another time when—"

"Who are those flowers for?" Ruby asked. "Did you bring them for Sara?"

"*Ne*, not Sara." Joseph's face grew hot. He tried to say, "I brought them for you," but again the words stuck in his throat. Dumbly, he held them out to her. It took every ounce of his courage not to turn and run.

Don't miss
A GROOM FOR RUBY
by Emma Miller, available August 2017 wherever
Love Inspired® books and ebooks are sold.

www.LoveInspired.com

Reward the book lover in you!

Earn points from all your Harlequin book purchases from wherever you shop.

Turn your points into *FREE BOOKS* of your choice
OR
EXCLUSIVE GIFTS from your favorite authors or series.

Join for FREE today at
www.HarlequinMyRewards.com.

Harlequin My Rewards is a free program (no fees) without any commitments or obligations.

MYR17